A
DANGEROUS
TIME

murder, mystery and suspense

BUD CRAIG

Paperback published by The Book Folks

London, 2019

© Bud Craig

ISBN 978-1-0946-6358-6

www.thebookfolks.com

PART ONE

INTO THE GREAT WIDE OPEN

CHAPTER ONE

Dawn walked through the village in the afternoon sunshine, visibly relaxing with every step, despite the heavy bag she was carrying. Half term next week. Seven days away from Alderton Academy: no learning journeys; no demanding ten year-olds; no stroppy parents. Tomorrow she'd get on her bike and just ride. She had only the vaguest idea where she was going, but by lunchtime she'd be miles away, ready for anything.

Her phone cut short her holiday fantasies. She stopped to put her bag down before answering.

"Hello, Dawn, coming out to play?"

She pursed her lips, letting out a deep sigh.

"How many more times? I've already told you..."

"Oh, Dawn, don't be like that."

"What do you not understand about 'I don't want to see you again'?"

"You know you don't mean that..."

"You'll soon find out whether I mean it or not. The last time was your final warning. You know what I'm going to do."

"You won't be doing anything. It would be very unwise..."

She ended the call. God, why should she have to put up with this creep? No point in worrying about it now. She walked on until she arrived at her sister's house and let herself in. Nice of Michelle to go away at such a convenient time. She went into the spare bedroom, dumping her bag on an armchair. Put him out of your mind, Dawn, don't let him get to you. She went to the bathroom and had a shower, washing away her tension.

Back in the bedroom ten minutes later, she was calm again. From the bag she took out her motorbike gear. As she got dressed, she thought about the dream she'd had two nights ago about Ed coming back. He had looked exactly the same except for his hair, which had turned completely white. Had it been an anxiety dream? A warning of some kind that her husband would return and spoil everything? It had disturbed and intrigued Dawn in equal measure.

What would Ed really be like now, wherever he was? In two years and a bit he couldn't have changed that much. Maybe a little greyer, heavier with all that beer he drank. When he first left, she had convinced herself he would return to her one day. It had taken nearly three months to face up to the truth: Ed would never come back.

What a fool she'd been to invest so much in her marriage, make it the centre of everything. While her friends had thrown themselves into a life of wall-to-wall pleasure, she'd been settling down, becoming middle-aged. Edward Fraser, or rather her obsession with him, had robbed her of her youth, so she set about recapturing it. Cashing in her life insurance and buying the Harley Davidson had been just the start. Going blonde had been next. The new image had caused a bit of a stir in the closed community of Alderton, though the kids at school had considered it 'dead cool'.

At that point she had only ever been with one man. Ridiculous to think of that now. She had put that right on her first trip away on the bike. After that there was no stopping her. Finding someone looking for a discreet dalliance was all too easy. As long as the sex was good, that was what mattered. She was finished with love and marriage and all that rubbish. She just wanted to have some fun.

She looked in the mirror for a final check. It was the leather look today – she knew he liked it. Skin-tight trousers, a biker's jacket complete with zips and studs over a Hells Angels T-shirt. A touch of make-up and she was all set. Looking good, she said to her reflection. Blondes definitely had more fun. All the dressing up, the games of make believe, the taking on of a new persona helped her throw off the inhibitions that had held her back for too long.

And what about you, Ed? Would you like what you see? Or would you tell me not to be stupid? Strange seeing an Ed look-alike yesterday. The bloke nipping into the Market Tavern in Loventon as she came out of Dustin's department store could have been him, though she'd only caught a fleeting glimpse. Whether it was him or not, it made no difference. She'd taken the final steps towards getting Ed out of her life once and for all. When she got back from holiday, she just had to sign a couple of documents and she wouldn't need to think about him anymore.

At Michelle's kitchen table later, Dawn sipped an ice cold beer, while preparing a snack for later. She placed Lovendale blue on the cheese board then looked in the knife drawer where she came across one of those cheese wires with wooden handles attached. She opened a packet of Bath Olivers and arranged a few of them on a plate next to a bottle of red wine.

Picking up the remote control she switched on the TV, tuning into the BBC news channel. Quentin Diplock, one of the few people from the North East to get any national coverage, was posing dramatically outside Lovendale Cathedral. He was retiring soon. Good riddance, she said to herself, although a good Christian girl like her shouldn't be saying such things about the Bishop of Lovendale.

Oh, shouldn't she? That depended on what you called Christian. Certainly not Diplock's Old Testament, hellfire and damnation philosophy. As Quentin began reminiscing about life in a parish in Greater Manchester ten years ago, Dawn switched off. She turned to the paperback she had bought the other day. A signed copy no less.

Dawn's mobile beeped before she had got past page one. She was about to read the text message when she heard the back door opening and footsteps coming towards her. She turned to see who it was, a smile on her face.

"Oh, it's you," she said, her voice thick with disappointment.

CHAPTER TWO

I didn't know it at the time, but that Friday night in late May when I went into the lounge of the Carpenters Arms in Bentley was when it all kicked off. I walked past a notice board with posters advertising a book signing by Richard Keppler – I'd missed him, whoever he was – an Elvis tribute act and an evening with the North East's leading clairvoyant. A quick look at my watch told me it was ten past eight.

I had checked in three quarters of an hour previously, sticky with sweat and sun cream, having walked eleven miles. A shower had had its usual semi-miraculous effect and now I felt human again. Despite being tee-total most of the time, tonight I really fancied a pint. Probably because earlier in the evening I'd passed the local brewery with its big red sign advertising Bentley Original Bitter next to a foaming tankard.

I saw Paddy McCann CBE standing at the bar, talking to Clive Wheatley. Both were dressed for golf. I asked myself which outfit was more lacking in aesthetic appeal: Paddy's grey V-neck pullover with yellow and pink diamonds or Clive's sickly green polo shirt and red and black check trousers? The branch chairman of the local

Labour Party and the left-wing vicar of Alderton in Lovendale were clearly competing for the *Garish Gear Trophy*.

I heard Clive raise his voice, but at first I was too far away to make out what he was saying. Paddy coughed and, trying to placate his companion, made calming gestures with his hands like a choirmaster instructing the singers to lower the volume. Even that amount of movement made him wheeze. He was only a couple of years older than me but a lifetime of smoking and drinking had taken its toll. When I got nearer the bar, he greeted me like I was his best friend.

"Sam, good to see you, mate."

Relief that I had interrupted a tricky conversation was written all over Paddy's face. Clive plonked his glass of red wine on the bar counter almost hard enough to break it.

"I'm warning you, McCann," he shouted, waving a fist, "I won't be responsible for my actions if you don't..."

Despite his anger, Clive still managed to speak in a precise, vicarish way; his northern accent was still in evidence but had been modified at his private school. At this point the man of God, presumably deciding actions spoke louder than words, tried to land a right hook on Paddy's jaw. Clive nearly swung himself off his feet but missed his target. Just as well: Clive wasn't particularly tall or heavy – about average, I'd say – but there'd been enough weight behind the punch to lay anybody out flat.

"Take it easy, mate," said Paddy, "people are watching."

In fact, nobody was taking a blind bit of notice. The scrum of people trying to get a drink had their backs to us and the bar staff were too busy. Diners continued to eat their meals from the *Early Bird Menu,* tried to choose between sticky toffee pudding and Eton mess or stared gormlessly at their phones. Clive's arms now hung by his side; he flexed his fingers as if preparing for another assault. So far, he hadn't favoured me with any sort of greeting. Taking his wine from the bar, he scowled morosely and scratched what little hair he had left. Baldness had struck Clive in his twenties, about the time he was starting to go grey.

"If you'll excuse me, Sam," said Clive.

With that, he polished off his drink, slammed the glass down on the bar again – still leaving it intact – and stormed out without another word. Paddy shook his head.

"I could do with a drink after that. What are you having, Sam?"

"Pint of BOB, please."

Paddy turned to the bar to order my beer and a Scotch for himself. What was going on? I somehow didn't think the Reverend Wheatley had been trying to save Paddy's soul.

"Clive didn't seem very happy," I said.

"A combination of booze and golf. Guaranteed to bring out the worst in people."

Two men in their forties coming to blows over a game? Possible. But Clive the worse for drink? Unlikely. Both Paddy and Clive thought they were important: being men in positions of power, both thought they were right all the time. That was probably at the heart of it. In any case, Paddy wasn't gonna confide in a mere acquaintance.

"You're not a golfer, are you, Sam?"

"Too busy playing cricket, Paddy. Plus, I can't wear pastels, they make me look all washed out."

He chuckled and passed my glass.

"Perish the thought. Anyway, you can't be too busy to play golf. You can just do nine holes like me and Clive tonight. Only takes a couple of hours."

"Three hours too long in other words."

"You're quick, I'll give you that. We need people like you on the council."

"Anything but that, Paddy."

I took my first mouthful of beer and thought of what I knew about McCann. He was leader of Lovenshire County

Council, sat on the board of Avanatta Phones, and had a stake in the Alderton Hall Hotel. Fingers in pies, that was Paddy. I could never have said what exactly he did, but I'd always thought he had a deep love of money. I recalled my dad's words about him: 'I wouldn't trust him as far as I could hoy him.'

"What brings you here anyway, Sam?"

I took another sip of beer.

"I'm doing the Lovendale Way. Just finished the third leg. Thought I'd treat myself to a night in a posh hotel."

"You do right. Are you on your own, like?"

"Yeah, I needed to get away from everyone."

He nodded. It wouldn't take long to work out I was trying to escape from thoughts of Nadia. I'd wondered at first whether walking in the area where I'd lived all my life was a good idea, but I didn't have the time or money to go further afield. In any case I'd soon realised I had made the right decision. Minutes after walking out of my door I felt as if I were miles away. And the North East of England was at its best in the summer. Plenty of daylight.

"You're looking well off it."

Much to my surprise I felt well. Covering seventy-two miles in six days had been my only goal. That had taken my mind off my broken marriage as well as keeping me in shape. Maybe I should write a book: *Fitness for Cuckolds*. Paddy knocked back his whisky.

"Well, I'd better be on my way. The wife's picking me up, mustn't be late. Look after yourself."

"You too, Paddy."

"Oh, by the way, is it next week you're doing my kitchen?"

"Yeah, Thursday, I think it is."

"The one we've got now seems OK to me, but you know what women are like, don't you?"

Judging by all the affairs he'd had, Paddy should be a leading expert.

"I wish I did," I said.

* * *

The next morning, just after nine, I got stuck into an
excellent full English and read *The Lovendale Chronicle*.
Quentin Diplock, 'the controversial cleric', was still
hogging the headlines. As I read, I thought about the near
punch up I had witnessed. It had its funny side, especially
as an Anglican priest had struck the first blow or tried to.
At the same time, the incident disturbed me. What had
caused Clive to behave like that? I'd probably never know,
which was just as well. I had enough problems of my own.

* * *

Two days later, on the bank holiday Monday, I had
nearly finished the final leg. Around seven in the evening I
tramped along the top of Swanny Fell, just steady away,
one foot in front of the other, feeling every one of my
forty-three years. My iPod played a Beethoven symphony
to help me on my way. I wallowed in the majesty of the
Pastoral, admiring the way it was put together. Clever lad,
that Ludwig. Earlier in the day I had had a bit of bop to
Status Quo, relived my teenage years with Deacon Blue's
greatest hits and was soothed by *In A Silent Way*. Miles
Davis – another clever clogs.

I watched sheep clambering up the hillside as the
evening sun gradually nudged aside a bank of pale cloud;
the river Loven twisted rapidly over the rocks in the valley
hundreds of feet below; a steam train chugged along. The
honey smell of cut grass mingled with the fragrance of
May blossom and wild garlic. A lark warbled up ahead,
blending with the quee-quee of a curlew in the distance.
Everything was lovely, except for an overweight woman
ahead of me letting her Labrador run free, ignoring the
signs warning owners to control their dogs to protect the
sheep. Typical.

"You're supposed to keep it on a lead," I said as I
overtook her.

"She's doing no harm. How would you like to be dragged round on a lead..."

"My sex life is no concern of yours, madam."

No concern of anyone's as it was non-existent. I put on a spurt to get well away before she could reply. Then my mobile rang.

"Is that Sam?"

"Oh, hiya, Penny."

What could she want? Had she decided to have the vicarage done up?

"Have you seen Dawn?"

"Dawn?"

I sat down on a convenient bench. I looked down at the dust that had settled on my orange socks.

"Yes, Dawn Fraser."

I pictured Penny in jeans and one of her seemingly endless collection of T-shirts – a contrast with her power-dressing days before she and Clive had adopted Jacob. She'd given up her job with Avanatta, halting her steady climb up the management hierarchy.

Since she'd become a full-time mother and vicar's wife, it was as if, like an actress, she had changed to fit in with her new role. Instead of being all dynamic and in-your-face, she tried not to draw attention to herself. With her ginger hair and strong Midlands accent that was a tough task.

"Should I have?"

Too late, I realised that was an annoying way of not answering the question.

"I've been trying to get hold of her about the choir, but she's not returning my calls."

Why not drop a note through her letterbox? Now the helpless little woman, she was ready to panic at the least provocation. If I had a quid for each time she'd called round asking me to do a little job, I'd be well off.

"Sorry, I can't help you."

"It's unlike her, she's normally so reliable. I hope she's all right."

"I'm sure she is, Penny."

"Ah, well, I'll just keep trying. Clive's away at the moment which doesn't help."

This was a common complaint from Penny.

"Yeah?"

"He's on an SR seminar in Castlebridge."

"SR?"

"Spiritual Renewal. Clive reckons SR has the power to rejuvenate the soul."

"Right."

She apologised for disturbing me and rang off. As I walked on, I remembered it was half-term. Dawn would be away; she'd have her phone switched off most of the time. Problem solved. Penny was worrying over nothing. Perhaps she needed a bit of SR. I wondered if the seminar would stop Clive attacking people who upset him. Did Penny know about his attempted assault on Paddy? I suspected not.

Clive wasn't a close friend but we'd been in the same class at primary school. After that he moved in different circles: boarding school, Cambridge University, the Church of England, various jobs around the country. Around three years ago, he'd returned to the north east from a post near Leicester, where he had met Penny.

As I saw Loven Terrace ahead, I thought of my neighbour, Michelle. I'd miss her when she went off to work in New York. Her house-sitter would be moving in tomorrow. What did they call her? It began with K, I knew that. An ex-copper from London, wasn't she? Never been north of Watford before. I only hoped she wasn't one of those who expressed incredulity about how nice it was up here. Michelle had asked me to look after her. How was I meant to do that? Remembering her name wouldn't be a bad start... Kate, that was it.

CHAPTER THREE

Kate pulled into the kerb, listened to the last few seconds of *Into the Great Wide Open* and checked the dashboard clock. Six fifteen. She hadn't made bad time. Picking up her handbag from the passenger seat, she got out and stretched her stiff muscles. Enjoying the feel of the sun on her face, she admired the ivy-clad Georgian town house: her home for the foreseeable future. Reading the FOR SALE sign, she tried to remember the estate agent's blurb she'd read online: '...a beautifully preserved terrace in a much sought after riverside location in the traditional village of Alderton'. The cost of a house like this was a fraction of what it would fetch in the south east, but Michelle wasn't expecting it to sell quickly.

Kate had another stretch and locked the Mini. She thought back to the last time Michelle had visited her in Kew and brought up the house-sitting idea. Over a bottle of Prosecco, they had discussed the pros and cons ad infinitum without reaching a conclusion. Michelle had boosted Lovendale with a will. At one stage she'd said:

"You might meet someone really nice. Just imagine lying on a windswept hillside being ravished by a monosyllabic northerner."

Had that clinched it? Kate smiled at the thought. It was a nice fantasy. She had had to get by on fantasy lately. Would she ever have sex again? Moving onto more practical things, she texted Michelle to say she'd arrived. Then she strolled with a lazy elegance towards the shop a few yards away. Her shorts showed off long, tanned legs. Before she'd set out on her journey, she'd wondered if a woman rapidly approaching her fortieth birthday should wear shorts. Or a sleeveless T-shirt, or have long hair; or be allowed out in public for that matter. Charles had always said she looked fantastic, whatever her age, but that was in the good old days.

'Into the great wide open, under a sky of blue', Tom Petty had sung. Spot on so far, Tom. Hardly able to believe she had been two hundred and fifty miles away that morning, she was thrown by the unnatural quiet. She sniffed at a pungent aroma of animal matter, which seemed to say, 'you're in the country now'.

A young couple in replica football shirts walked hand in hand into the Bricklayers Arms a little way down the street. The sign just past the pub saying 'Alderton Cricket Club 1/2 a mile' conjured up a picture of spectators picnicking on the boundary edge as a match unfolded slowly in the sunshine. She suddenly felt a long way from home. At least here, she told herself, she wouldn't run the risk of bumping into Charles. Or Daddy.

On the outskirts of the village, she had seen signs telling passing motorists Lovendale was an area of outstanding natural beauty. In case one hadn't noticed, presumably. It was stunning all right and Alderton was an archetypal English village, one of the prettiest she had ever seen. Yet this was *The North*. As she grappled with this apparent contradiction, her mobile beeped. A text from Michelle:

> *Glad you got there OK. Sorry I'm not around to welcome you. Should be back tomorrow afternoon. Oh, forgot to tell you. Tomorrow morning a neighbour*

is picking up some stuff for a jumble sale from the shed. She has a key so no need to stay in. M xxx

Kate followed a tattooed woman wheeling a pushchair into the shop past the newspapers on display by the door. Picking up a wire basket, she glanced without much interest at the headlines about *Strictly*, the latest unemployment figures and immigration. She put a copy of the local paper in her basket.

She went over to the dairy section where a woman wearing blue overalls splattered with paint chatted to a tall, fair-haired man with a bottle of Malbec in his hand. Kate looked him up and down, trying not to stare. Picking up a plastic bottle of semi-skimmed, she listened, fascinated, enjoying the lilting rhythm of their speech.

"He's doing great, it's his birthday tomorrow," said the female decorator.

"You having a party?"

"Yeah, ten two-year-olds."

"Best of luck with that."

"I'll need it. Anyway, Sam, I'd better be off. May see you Thursday," she said.

"Yeah, see you, Tiffany."

Tiffany walked over to the tills. A woman of about Kate's age came in, her high heels clacking on the laminated flooring. She stopped suddenly, undoing the jacket of her business suit.

"Attention, please, ladies and gentlemen," she half shouted, "I have an announcement to make."

The seven or eight people in the store abandoned their shopping to look at her.

"Great news. Brian has finally got his leg over with Tiffany."

Everyone turned towards the post office section at the far end, where a balding man with a paunch looked from side to side in desperation, as though searching for a hiding place.

"Last night I caught them at it in the cricket pavilion. Not a pretty sight."

"Shut it, Rebecca," said Tiffany.

Rebecca ignored the interruption.

"I'm particularly pleased for Tiffany, because my husband was the only man in Lovendale she hadn't shagged."

Tiffany, red in the face, slammed her basket down on the check-out and bustled over to her traducer.

"Pack it in now," she demanded.

"Oh, I've not finished yet, my girl."

Tiffany moved dangerously close.

"Finished? I'll finish you, Lumley, you cow," she snarled, trying to claw at Rebecca's face with long, purple nails.

Rebecca stepped back as Tiffany screamed into her face.

"Toxic bitch! You're dead, you."

Gripping her by the shoulders, she gave Rebecca an almighty shove, causing her to barge into Kate, who was knocked flying by the impact. The last things she remembered were the top coming off the milk, an apologetic murmur from Rebecca, and her head hitting the corner of a chest freezer.

* * *

Kate heard two women talking.

"Is she all right?"

"If she is, it's no thanks to you."

She kept her eyes tight shut. A man spoke.

"Don't try to move."

Wincing at the pain in her head, she decided to follow his advice for now at least. It took a few seconds to remember what had happened. No wonder her head hurt.

"You were unconscious for a bit," said the same voice. "Need to be careful. How are you feeling?"

Disoriented and nauseous, she could have said.

18

"Not sure."

"Don't worry, we've called an ambulance."

Oh, no, a fine start to her new life. Kate risked opening her eyes. Rebecca was wiping milk from her skirt with a tissue; Tiffany was glaring at her as though it were all her fault; Sam, the Malbec man, was leaning over her solicitously. Attempting a smile, she was sick over her new top.

* * *

"This is awfully good of you, Sam," said Kate at about eleven the next morning as they walked through the hospital car park.

They stopped when they reached a white van with *Sam Flint Kitchen King* painted on the side. Sam unlocked it.

"I had to come out this way. Think nothing of it."

"That's the last thing I'll do," she said, getting into the van, "considering you came with me to hospital in the ambulance."

"Like I say, it was no bother, really."

"No bother? If you hadn't promised the nurses you'd keep an eye on me, I'd still be on ward 23."

"Well, somebody needs to watch out for signs of concussion, don't they?" he said, switching on the engine and reversing out of the parking space.

"When I arrived in Alderton yesterday," said Kate, "I was sure nothing ever happened there. Yet I've already been caught up in a fight and hospitalised."

Sam pulled out onto the main road.

"Appearances can be deceptive, Kate. As well as your bit of bother, there's the case of the vicar and the council leader."

"What?"

In no time they were passing through rolling countryside. Sam kept her entertained for the rest of the short journey by telling her the story of Paddy and Clive. A few minutes later they reached Loven Terrace. The van pulled up at the kerb.

"You must come in for a coffee," she said, looking down to collect the handbag at her feet.

Sam spoke at the same time.

"What's going on here?"

There was a kind of barrier on the pavement outside number 13. Blue and white tape saying *Police Line Do Not Cross* was strung across it.

"Oh, my God. I don't believe it."

Just inside the barrier, a man in a protective suit was on his mobile phone.

"Too early to be sure," he was saying.

Kate got out of the van and approached the guy with the phone as he ended his call.

"Excuse me."

"I'm sorry, madam, you can't come in here, it's a ..."

"But I... I'm meant to be staying here, the owner is a friend of mine."

He looked at her appraisingly, a puzzled expression on his face.

"The owner? That would be?"

He sounded sceptical.

"Michelle Thomas."

"I see. And you are?"

"Kate George."

"Ah, the house-sitter. I'm Detective Sergeant Adam Penrose, Lovendale CID. I'm afraid only authorised personnel are allowed in the house for the time being."

Just then, Sam got out of the van and joined them.

"What's up?"

"Well, Mr..."

Sam told Penrose his name. The sergeant repeated the explanation he'd given Kate.

"Does Michelle know about this?" she asked.

"Of course. She'll be returning home as soon as possible. In the meantime, is there somewhere you could wait?"

Kate and Sam exchanged a glance.

"We could go to my place," he suggested. "Have a cup of coffee."

"Suits me. Thanks. You will keep me informed, Sergeant?"

"Sure, but it may be some time. Where can we find you?"

"At number nine," said Sam.

Penrose went back into Michelle's house.

"I'll be helping the police with their inquiries," said Kate as they approached Sam's front door. "It'll be a new experience, if nothing else."

* * *

"Sorry it's taken so long," said Sergeant Penrose a couple of hours later.

The three of them sat at a picnic table with fresh cups of coffee. Flower pots and hanging baskets brightened the faded red brick and dull, grey flagstones of Sam's back yard. It would have been pleasant sitting in the sunshine in different circumstances.

"I'll explain what this is all about. A body was found in the shed of Ms Thomas's house at seven this morning."

"A body?"

Kate's eyes were drawn to Sam's shed in a corner of the yard. He'd told her earlier he used it as an office. One hoped there'd be nothing more sinister in there than a desk and a laptop.

"We believe the deceased to be a local teacher called Dawn Fraser."

"Dawn, oh, no," said Sam, turning to Kate. "She's Michelle's sister."

"Oh, my God."

"You obviously know her, Mr Flint," said the DS.

Sam nodded, taking a deep breath.

"Yeah. She used to teach my daughter. Emily will be gutted."

"I'm sorry to be bringing you such sad news. I'm afraid I can't tell you much more as it's so early in our investigation. At the minute, we consider it an unexplained death."

"Ms George, did you know Mrs Fraser?"

"No. Michelle often talked about her sister, but I never actually met her."

DC Penrose turned his attention back to Sam.

"How well did you know Dawn Fraser, Mr Flint?"

Sam cleared his throat before speaking.

"Fairly well, I suppose."

"Did you see her socially?"

"I used to. She was married to a friend of mine. Still is, legally, as far as I know, but Ed left her a couple of years ago."

"Where is he now?"

"No idea."

"When did you last see Mrs Fraser?"

"Not sure. She hasn't been to the house for a while. I see her in the village now and again. I hadn't seen her for a few days before I went away."

"We're looking at the period from last Friday to today. Did you see anything unusual?"

Sam considered this for a moment.

"Well, last Friday I was in the middle of the Lovendale Way. I'd got to Bentley by then, I think. I got back home on Monday evening. I can't say I noticed anything out of the ordinary."

The detective soon ran out of questions and got up to leave.

"When can I move into the house?" Kate asked.

"Not until tomorrow morning, I'm afraid."

"I was hoping to move in today."

"Sorry."

"I suppose I'd better find a B&B or something," said Kate after the DS left.

"One of my holiday flats is free at the minute," said Sam, "you can stay the night there. The couple who were staying this week had to go home early."

"If you're sure..."

"Course. Give Michelle a call and tell her she can stay there with you."

"That's very nice of you. I'll pay of course."

"Don't be daft. You can tell all your friends how fantastic it is, drum up a bit of custom."

She gave him her nicest smile.

"That's a promise. How do you come to have a holiday apartment?"

"I bought an old house a few years back. An old woman had lived in it and it was practically falling down. When she died the family couldn't wait to get rid of it."

"And you did it up?"

"Yeah, turned it into two flats. Lap of luxury."

"Great. You must come and eat with us. Is there a decent take-away round here?"

"There's the best fish and chip shop in the world."

"Great."

Sam looked at his watch.

"I'm sorry. I've got to nip out and see someone. It shouldn't take more than half an hour."

When he'd gone and she was alone with her thoughts, a mixture of shock and sadness threatened to overwhelm Kate. To think she'd been feeling so positive before Penrose's return. Meeting Sam had been a big plus. What she had seen of him so far, she liked. While waiting for the police to come back, they'd had toasted sandwiches and chatted amiably enough. They'd discovered a mutual love of cricket – he was captain of the village side and offered to 'put a word in' when she applied to join. At that moment she had made up her mind to enjoy her time in the north. Now she wasn't so sure.

CHAPTER FOUR

Just after I came back from my appointment, Penny Wheatley came round. Jacob was with her, fast asleep in his pushchair. It was still only half two. Surely with everything that had happened, it must be six o'clock by now.

"Oh, Sam, can I speak to you for a moment; it's quite urgent."

"Sure, come in."

I thought the urgent problem was a leaky tap or something, until I saw her hands were trembling and she looked as if she'd been crying.

"This is Kate, Michelle's house-sitter," I said as we went into the back yard.

After a mumbled greeting, she joined us at the table, the pushchair by her side, where Jacob slept on.

"Dawn Fraser is dead," she said.

"Yes, I..."

"I found her body."

"Oh, no," I said, "I've had the police round but they didn't tell me much."

"I hope you don't mind my calling," said Penny, pulling at the sleeves of her jumper, "but I had to talk to somebody."

"Must have been terrible."

"I should say it was. I'm sure I won't sleep tonight."

"Is Clive still away?" I asked.

She nodded.

"That made it worse. If only we hadn't moved up here. We were perfectly happy in Winwood, but Clive had to come home because of..."

She paused, took a deep breath and went on.

"I went round to Michelle's house this morning to collect some stuff for the church jumble sale. That would have been around ten, just after I dropped Jacob off at playgroup."

She twisted her hands together on her lap.

"I had a key for the shed door but it was unlocked. I switched on the light. As you'll find out, Kate, it's impossible to see a thing in there without a light on, no matter what time of day it is."

Penny had always gone on a bit but today she could be forgiven.

"I noticed nothing untoward at first. I had helped Michelle to clear out all the heavy things – furniture and what have you – about ten days ago. You wouldn't believe what was dumped in there, a bedside table, an old laptop, a suitcase..."

She stopped what she was saying, whether because she realised its irrelevance or because it was all getting too difficult, I couldn't tell. Penny shook her head gently and seemed about to cry but managed to continue.

"I knew the things I wanted were in the far corner and when I went over there, I saw Dawn wearing her motor-bike leathers. She was sort of dangling by a rope from a kind of rafter – not the right word, I know, but..."

God, no wonder Penny was in shock. She rubbed at her hands as if she were cold.

"Rafter's as good a word as any, we know what you mean, Penny," said Kate kindly.

"I'm afraid it looks as if Dawn took her own life," said Penny.

Dawn kill herself? I couldn't believe it.

"I didn't scream like they do on TV. I just stood there, fixed to the spot... I went closer and soon realised she was dead..."

She paused, biting her bottom lip and staring at a cup on the table.

"So I dialled 999 and..."

"How come she was in the shed?" I asked.

Penny sat up and picked up the threads of her story.

"I don't know. Dawn was meaning to pop into Michelle's house last Friday to get the place ready for you, Kate. She was going away the next morning and of course Michelle was in Edinburgh for a few days."

"Did you see Dawn that day?"

"No, the police asked me that. I had taken Jacob to my mother's."

Had Dawn been in the shed since Friday? What an awful thought. When Penny left, Kate sat deep in thought for a while. This must have hit her hard.

* * *

"We were never that close – well, you know that, Sam," said Michelle about half seven that night, "but she was my sister."

Michelle, Kate and I were sitting round the dining room table of the holiday apartment. The remains of our fish and chips littered the table. The two women had made steady inroads into a bottle of Sauvignon Blanc – I'd limited myself to my usual one glass.

"Dawn was... well, the only word I can think of is 'respectable'. She spent all her life in this village. Her ambitions were straightforward: to be a teacher and get married and live happily ever after in Lovendale."

Over grey trousers Michelle wore a dark green, baggy T-shirt, the kind favoured by overweight, out of condition people everywhere. In contrast, Kate's cotton trousers and stylish red top only showed how fit she was. In both senses of the word.

"Dawn only had one boyfriend before Ed. She said she knew from the start she wanted to settle down with him. How could she?"

Michelle sniffed, wiped away a tear and squared her shoulders as if to show she was determined to carry on.

"They were married at twenty, didn't even live together beforehand. It was madness. Ed became practically her whole life. She didn't want kids. She once said to me, 'what do we need children for, we have each other?'"

"Too good to last," I suggested.

Michelle nodded in agreement.

"I reckon in the end Ed felt stifled. Can't say I blame him. He bailed out two years ago without leaving a forwarding address."

"How did she react to Ed going?" asked Kate.

"For a while she carried on as normal. Then after couple of months she bought a motorbike and dyed her hair blonde. You remember, don't you, Sam?"

"It was the talk of the village for a while," I said, "but people got used to it."

"The funny thing was," said Michelle, "Dawn's life went on the same. She carried on being a pillar of the church."

More wine, a deep breath and on she went.

"She sang in the choir and everything. Her attachment to the church increased after Ed left. She did the flowers, edited the parish newsletter, volunteered for every village committee going."

It was easy to mock people like Dawn Fraser, but she never did anybody any harm and she got something out of all those activities.

"I got away from here as soon as I could," Michelle went on. "Oh, I came back a couple of years ago because mum was ill. I felt I should help Dawn out. Once mum died, I started looking for another job."

Two deaths in the family within a few months. Hard to take.

"How had she been feeling lately?" asked Kate.

"The same as usual, as far as I know. We didn't have, you know, sisterly heart-to-hearts, Dawn wasn't into all that."

She took a tissue from a box on the table and wiped a tear from her cheek.

"She was happy, I know she was, she must have been. She can't have killed herself."

* * *

After a while Kate got up to make coffee.

"What do you think of Kate then?" asked Michelle.

"She seems nice."

"Yes, one of the best. We met when I was Director of Finance for the Metropolitan Police."

"Yeah, she mentioned that."

"Kate's had a bad time lately, Sam. Marriage break-up, well, you can relate to that. Charles, her husband, is a top barrister, absolutely loaded. Also an arrogant shit, between you and me."

I wondered if Kate would want me to know all this, but once Michelle had got going there was no stopping her.

"I mean, you'd think any man would be happy with someone like Kate. She's kind, considerate, intelligent. And drop-dead gorgeous."

She was a canny looking lass all right.

"But that's not enough for Charlie boy. It didn't help that Kate couldn't have kids."

She sighed and said no more for a while. I had no idea what to say in reply to this deeply personal information. It was just as well Kate returned from the kitchen before Michelle could go into more detail.

CHAPTER FIVE

In the early hours of Thursday morning, Kate switched the bedside light back on and looked at her alarm clock. Two forty-five. She had lain in bed since one o'clock, her head bursting with the events of the last two days. There was just too much to think about. Michelle for a start. She must be going through hell.

And what about Sam? The poor guy had been landed with a kind of support role. He must be cursing the day he volunteered to help the woman from London who had arrived in the village to cause havoc. From now on, he would steer well clear.

She'd hoped to turn life in the Met into a fading memory. And now this. Instead of her going to work, the work was coming to her, making it impossible to forget about what had once been her career.

Since she had decided to leave London, a voice inside her head had kept telling her she was just running away. If Charles were still with her, would she have packed in her job and accepted Michelle's offer? Of course not. Things would have gone on in the same safe, predictable way.

The day he'd dumped her invaded her mind once again. She wished she could stop these flashbacks. *The thing is, darling, I've met somebody else.* To call her darling at a time like that. Then the real punch in the guts: his twenty-something bit of stuff was pregnant. Rub salt in the wound, why don't you? What kind of father would Charles make? His new love must be eight months gone by now.

"Enough!" she shouted to the ceiling.

Kate was beginning to see a pattern in her life. Dropping out of Oxford University coincided with boyfriend problems. So much for being a strong, independent woman. It couldn't have been just that, surely. There were lots of things that conspired to drive her away: the self-satisfied types she'd met who flaunted their privilege; the idea she was simply doing what was expected of her; being sick of essays and exams. The boyfriend was long forgotten. She even struggled to remember his name. It was either Jonathan or Josh. Or was it Jake? Forgetting Charles' name might be a touch more difficult.

A broken marriage had earned her membership of a club nobody really wanted to join. When Michelle had been going through the same thing, Kate had been full of sympathy, never dreaming she would be in the same position before long. Getting out the other side, that was her aim or so she told herself. The escape to Lovendale had been part of that but murder definitely wasn't. What a mess.

How would Daddy react to all this? With a mixture of shock, disapproval and 'I told you so' smugness as if it were Kate's fault for not taking paternal advice. Advice? More like instructions. Kate loved her father – didn't everybody? – but she was glad to be away from his sphere of influence for a while.

As Kate turned on her side for the tenth time, her mind took her back to the death of Michelle's sister. There was a flaw in Penny Wheatley's account of finding Dawn's body. What was it that didn't make sense? Ten minutes later, she was no further forward. She switched off the light, determined to get to sleep. When she was on the point of dropping off, it came to her. She switched the light back on. The light, that was it... oh, no, that must mean...

She needed to go through it one more time. Penny had had to turn the shed light on before she went inside. That meant somebody switched the light off after Dawn was left hanging. Had Dawn wanted to commit suicide, she would have needed to switch the light on as otherwise, according to Penny, she wouldn't have been able to see a thing. Dawn would hardly have got down from the rope to switch it off. God. It didn't take a genius to work out what that meant. Kate tried to persuade herself she was reading too much into it, but she could only come to one conclusion: Dawn Fraser had been murdered.

CHAPTER SIX

At eight o'clock on the morning after Dawn's body was found, I was ready for work but thought I'd read the front-page article in the *Lovendale Chronicle* before leaving home:

Mystery of Popular Teacher's Death by Dale Wilson, Chief Reporter

Police are investigating the death of primary school Deputy Head, Dawn Fraser, after her body was found in a house in Loven Terrace, Alderton. Little is known of the details yet. Detective Sergeant Adam Penrose told the Chronicle that Lovendale police are treating it as an unexplained death. "We are asking anybody who was in the vicinity of Loven Terrace between Friday 27th May and Wednesday 1st June..."

At that point I had to get up to answer the door.

"Good morning, Sam," said a skinny, balding man in jeans and open-necked shirt.

"Well, if it isn't the chief reporter himself. Come in."

He followed me into the kitchen.

"Terrible about Dawn, wasn't it?" he said, joining me at the table.

I pointed to the paper.

"Yeah. Just been reading your piece."

He nodded.

"Not something I ever thought I'd write about. I can't believe it, I mean, Dawn Fraser... I remember when she was Dawn Thomas and I was going out with her."

"That was a while ago, Dale."

He picked up the paper from the table, puffing out his cheeks, and sighed.

"Yeah. I take it the police came to see you with it happening so near you."

"Yeah. They asked me all sorts of questions but I couldn't help them."

"What do you make of it all?"

"Hard to say."

"The police didn't give any hint of how they were thinking?"

"No."

Dale put the paper back down.

"She can't have killed herself, can she, Sam?"

"Seems unlikely to say the least."

Dale looked near to tears. He was keen on Dawn back when they were sixteen. I assumed he was over that, but something like this would bring back memories.

"I'm gonna have to report on any developments. It'll be hard, I can tell you. I'd sooner forget about it for now. I only called round to get the cricket news. What does skipper, Sam Flint, think about Alderton's chances in the top of the table clash with Castlebridge?"

After carefully noting down my expert analysis, Dale left. I pondered what had been happening in Lovendale. There seemed to be a lot going on at the minute: Paddy almost knocked out by Clive in the Carpenters; Kate actually knocked out in the village shop; now an unexplained death two doors away. What next?

* * *

"I still can't believe it," said Paddy McCann later that morning.

Paddy and I were dumping a cupboard door into a skip in his back garden. Scratching my nose, which always itched at such times, I turned towards him, holding a hand up to shield my eyes from the sun.

"Nor can I. It's hard to make sense of something like this. Dawn was so young."

Paddy took a drag from his cigarette, wiping his dusty hands on his jeans. He shifted his weight from one foot to the other.

"Terrible business."

He looked at his watch, flicking ash from his fag. Paddy was rich by any normal standards, but had volunteered to help with knocking out the old kitchen to keep the price down. He had chosen Tiffany, the cheapest decorator for miles around, for the same reason.

"Anyway, I'll have to love you and leave you. I'd better clean myself up and get changed. I've got a meeting at Avanatta soon."

I suspected he would prefer to be doing work like this rather than attending endless meetings.

"I must get a card for Michelle while I'm out. She must be gutted, poor lass."

"Yeah, it's tough for her. I'm sure she'd appreciate a card."

"I passed Michelle's house Friday afternoon on the way to the shop. To think at that very moment Dawn might have been... doesn't bear thinking about."

"Certainly doesn't."

"It seemed like another quiet day in Lovendale. Apart for some boy racer type in a flash car who fancied himself as Lewis Hamilton. Anyway, better be off."

"OK," I said. "I'll just clear up and then go and get the tiles."

He turned to go, then stopped.

"I've just thought, I ought to get in touch with the police."

"Oh?"

"Yeah, they're asking people who were in Loven Terrace between Friday and yesterday to come forward. I'll give them a ring later. Anyway, see you."

"Yeah, see you, Paddy."

As he walked away, I looked round the perfectly sculpted garden, about six times the size of my back yard. McCann might have a mansion facing Alderton village green and loads of money but I didn't envy him. I had never fancied a job where I had to wear a suit, especially on a day like this.

On the way out of Paddy's front door twenty minutes later, I wondered what Kate made of village life. As a newcomer, she must wonder what had hit her in more ways than one. I'd tried to keep an eye on her, as I had promised Michelle, but hadn't expected to be taking her to and from hospital or sitting with her while she fielded questions from the police. She'd been in CID herself, but never let on to Sergeant Penrose. Why was that? Maybe she'd moved up here to get away from all that. I had reached the van when Tiffany walked down the path towards me.

"Sam, how're you doing?"

She wore velvet trousers and a white T-shirt today, looking different in off-duty gear. For a single parent whose sole source of income was painting and decorating she had plenty of clothes. She never seemed to be short of money either.

"Not bad."

"I saw your missus yesterday."

"Yeah?"

"She mentioned that carry-on in the shop."

So Nadia had found out about that, had she? No surprise there. That meant she probably knew about me taking Kate to hospital.

"That woman from down south shouldn't have got in the way of a private fight. She ended up with a bump on the head for her trouble."

That was one way of looking at it.

"She seems OK now."

Tiff was overwhelmed with indifference at this news.

"I was hoping to have a quick word with Paddy. Is he in?"

"Yeah, but you'd better be quick. He's going out soon."

"I need to double-check the colour scheme," she explained. "Might negotiate a nice bonus while I'm there."

"Bonus from Paddy? You must be joking."

She gave me a sly grin.

"Ah, but I know things about him."

* * *

I was about to get in the van when I saw Clive Wheatley walking along the footpath that bisected the green. He came over and said hello, straightening the collar of his brown check shirt. A pointless thing to do but then I'd always thought Clive a bit nervy despite his efforts to appear laid back.

"Glad I caught you, Sam. I only got back late last night. Terrible about Dawn, wasn't it?"

"Tragic."

"It will affect the village deeply. That's what the church is for, to bring the community together, help everybody move on."

Did he have to make a speech about it? Wasn't he basically saying, 'murder's good for business'. And what did he mean by the community? It never seemed to include me. Clive went on, seeming not to notice whether I was listening or not.

"Penny seemed to think Dawn had taken her own life."

"She can't have. She was always so upbeat."

He gave me a sad smile.

"Sometimes these things are hard to understand."

"Suppose so. How's Penny? She's had quite a shock."

He shrugged.

"Oh, she'll be OK. She's strong."

That sounded a bit dismissive, but presumably Clive knew his own wife.

"I need to be off, Clive."

"Sure... actually there is one other thing I need to mention."

"What's that?"

"I just wanted to apologise."

"Apologise?"

"Yes, about that business in the Carpenters."

My mind was on other things so I didn't catch on straight away.

"Oh, right, see what you mean. No need to apologise. Didn't bother me."

He smiled ruefully, as I pictured him throwing a punch.

"Nice of you to take it that way. I was afraid it would be all over social media, whereas nobody seems to have noticed."

If anything, he sounded a bit disappointed.

"Anyway, Sam, at the time I was a bit stressed. Having a crisis of faith to be honest. I went straight from the Carpenters to the Holy Trinity Centre in Castlebridge. Spent a few days working through a raft of issues with like-minded people. That did the trick."

Good for you, Clive. After he'd gone on for far too long while I nodded politely – he and Penny were two of a kind – I managed to get away from him and get on with my job.

* * *

"Is Emily in?" asked Nadia that evening.

The way my soon to be ex-wife sat upright in an armchair in my living room as though ready to tackle some important task, seemed to sum up her serious attitude to life. She had always found it hard to relax, which maybe explained her problems. As ever, she was dressed in dark colours: a blue, long-sleeved top and black trousers.

"No, she's at work. She should be back in an hour."

This wasn't a good time to entertain visitors – I was still in my work clothes and could have done with a shower.

"I need to leave by half past."

No doubt it would be council business that would drag her away. Now she was deputy leader of Lovendale Council, politics played an even bigger part in her life.

"Well, if you could hang on until six o'clock..."

"No, sorry."

Always busy, that was Nadia. I was surprised she could find the time to call in – last week she'd been to some Labour Party gathering and I knew she'd been away over the bank holiday weekend. I noticed she'd had her brown hair cut into a kind of bob. New glasses too. Was this make-over for her new lover?

"Is Emily OK?" asked Nadia.

"In general, she's fine. Upset about Dawn Fraser."

"Yeah, that was sad."

Silence fell. Awkward – that was how we were whenever we met. It was hard to believe we were once so easy together. Were we going to sit here indefinitely, trying to think of things to say?

"By the way," she said, "how's the girlfriend?"

"Girlfriend?"

"The one you took to hospital the other day."

It wasn't surprising she had found out what happened to Kate, but why did she still want to know what I was doing?

"She's not my girlfriend and if she were it wouldn't be any of your business, would it?"

Nadia shrugged.

"Just wondered. Rebecca told me about the, er, incident in the shop. She just gets worse. Anything for attention, that's Rebecca Lumley."

Nadia spent so long on council work that it was easy to forget she had a day job with *Lumley and Finkle*, chartered accountants. Now she began searching for her keys. I noticed a packet of extra strong mints in her handbag and groaned inwardly. As if things weren't bad enough.

CHAPTER SEVEN

By five o'clock Kate and Michelle had been sitting in the living room of the holiday apartment for a couple of hours with their bags packed. Finally, Michelle's mobile rang. With a sigh of relief, she answered the call. When she'd finished, she turned to Kate.

"That was the police. We can get into the house now."

"Great."

"They'll give us a chance to settle in and then come to see me. They have some information."

* * *

"There have been some developments, Ms Thomas," said DS Penrose later. "I'm afraid it's not good news. Following further inquiries, we have come to the conclusion that we must treat your sister's death as suspicious."

"You mean she was murdered?" asked Michelle.

"I'm afraid it looks that way. Mrs Fraser didn't die where she was found."

"What...?" Michelle managed to say before the tears started. "But who could have...? No, no, it can't be right. It was bad enough her being dead but... this..."

The DS waited for Michelle to collect herself.

"Do you feel up to answering a few questions?"

"Yes, but first, just tell me... I have to ask this now, otherwise I'll...?"

"What Michelle means…," said Kate.

"It's OK, I know what she means," said Sergeant Penrose. "There's no evidence of sexual assault."

Michelle let go of the breath she'd been holding, then wiped away a tear. The sergeant paused to let the information sink in.

"Before we go any further, can I ask if you know where your sister's phone is. We haven't been able to locate it."

"She normally kept it with her," said Michelle.

"We'll just have to keep on looking. In the meantime, we are anxious to trace Mr Fraser," he said. "Can you help us with that?"

"No. As far as I know, nobody's heard from Ed since he left."

"That was approximately how long ago?"

"Two years, give or take."

The sergeant noted down the answers and looked at his notebook as if it would help him in some way.

"Can you tell me where you were during the past week?"

"You can't think..."

Michelle gave her friend an apprehensive glance. Kate nodded as if giving her permission to answer.

"I was in Edinburgh at a conference."

She gave details of the hotel she stayed at, on what dates, and the name of her boss, who would vouch for her.

"What about you, Inspector?" he said. "Are you able to help me?"

"There's no need for formality, Sergeant, I'm no longer an inspector. Just call me Kate."

"Well, Kate, you didn't tell me you were in the Met."

He sounded put out by this omission.

"Not relevant, is it? I'm a civilian now and I can't tell you how good it feels."

"Even so, if you have any insights, I'm sure you'll share them with me."

Kate tutted silently.

"I'm afraid I have no insights. I think it's more important for me to support Michelle right now."

"Quite. Michelle, my next question is a hard one for you to face up to, but can you think of anybody who might have wanted to harm Dawn?"

Michelle took a tissue from a box on the coffee table and wiped her nose.

"Nobody. Everyone loved Dawn."

"Did she have a boyfriend?"

Michelle shrugged.

"No, I don't know of anybody she was involved with since Ed left."

CHAPTER EIGHT

"Good morning, Emily," said Mark as she arrived at the Avanatta shop on Friday morning, "this lady wants to talk to you, she's from the police."

The twenty-something woman beside him had fair hair in a pony-tail and a welcoming smile. She showed her ID then shook Emily's hand.

"Detective Constable Lindsay Travis."

"Hi."

Emily straightened her glasses.

"It was only a matter of time before they caught up with you," said Mark with an annoying grin. "Don't say a word until your lawyer arrives."

She raised her eyebrows at his inane banter. He gave her a wink and she smiled.

"Shut up, Mark."

"Sorry to disturb you at work," said the detective, "I called at your home but you'd already left."

"Er, what's it about?"

"If we could find somewhere private to talk, I'll explain."

"Right, I'll leave you to it, guys," said Mark, "I need to go to the Castlebridge store to pick up some iPhones. Some divvy delivered them to the wrong place."

Emily took the officer into a store room at the back of the shop. They sat surrounded by boxes of phones. The detective took a notebook and pen from her leather bag and adopted a pose of relaxed concentration.

"It's about Dawn Fraser," she said. "I understand you knew her."

"Well, kind of. She taught me in primary school and she'd, like, stop and chat if she saw me in the village. It was terrible to hear somebody killed her."

"We're talking to anyone who knew Dawn or lives in Loven Terrace. The period we're interested in is from Friday 27th May to Wednesday 1st June. Did you see or hear anything unusual near where you live?"

"I don't think so."

"Right. Just think about what you were doing on those days. That might help."

"Well, Friday was my day off so I had a lie-in. I went into town in the afternoon... oh, I saw Mrs Fraser that day."

"I see. What time was that?"

"It was afternoon," she said, relieved to have remembered something, "around half four."

"And where was this?"

"At the bus stop opposite the shop in Alderton."

"Where were you going?"

"I was catching the bus to Loventon to see my therapist, but I can't see that being relevant, can you?"

"Quite. Getting back to Mrs Fraser, how did she seem?"

Emily shrugged.

"Much the same as usual."

"Usual?"

"Cheerful, chatty, dynamic. That's what she was like."

"She didn't seem to have anything on her mind?"

Emily shook her head.

"Was there anything unusual about her at all?"

"Not really."

"What was she wearing?"

For a moment Emily looked baffled.

"Not sure... oh, yes, a pink T-shirt, she often wore pink. And trousers, can't remember what colour. She had a bag with her."

"A bag?"

"Yeah, a sports bag I guess you'd call it. Like you'd take to the gym. The way she was carrying it I'd say it was pretty heavy."

DC Travis noted down what was said and considered it before moving on.

"Where was she going, did she say?"

"She was off to Michelle's house, her sister, you know. Said she had a few things to sort out there."

"Have you any idea what she'd be doing when she'd finished there?"

Emily thought for a moment.

"Only that she was going away the next morning, making an early start. She said she was just going to get on her bike and stop wherever she fancied."

"Was she any more specific about where she might go?"

"No, that was, like, the whole point. She wanted to make sure nobody could get in touch with her. I mean, she was a fantastic teacher and everything but I guess she had to get right away from it now and again."

"I see. How long were you chatting to her?"

"A couple of minutes. Then I was stuck at the bus stop for about half an hour, the 37 was late again."

"Did you see anybody else when you were there?"

"Three or four people went past as the bus left. The only one I recognised was Dale Wilson."

DC Travis looked up from her note-taking.

"And he is?"

"He's a friend of my dad's. I've known him all my life. He's a reporter for the Lovendale Chronicle."

"Oh, yeah, I know who you mean."

The constable wrote everything down. Emily thought she'd finished, but she had more questions.

"Do you know if there was a man in Dawn's life?"

"I didn't really know her well enough to say. I know her husband left a while ago."

"Right. Thank you."

"I don't know why you're thanking me. I can't see that anything I told you is any use."

She chewed her pen.

"On the contrary, it establishes that Dawn Fraser was alive on Friday afternoon. Nobody seems to have clapped eyes on her since."

* * *

After the detective had gone, Emily needed someone to talk to, but she'd have to wait until Mark got back. They had been an item for about eight months now. She'd never been out with somebody for so long before. He was dead good-looking but could be irritating. Still he was no more of a knob-head than any bloke. And he was nearly always cheerful – she needed someone like that to stop her brooding.

For the rest of the day on and off, Emily pondered the police interview. Had she really been the last person to see Mrs Fraser alive? The thought was strangely unsettling. Could meeting her at the bus stop be so significant? Whether it was or not, she had to get on with her job. A sudden influx of customers could have been considered a helpful distraction, but she would have liked a quiet ten minutes to analyse what had happened.

While selling a Samsung Galaxy to a fat, sweaty man who paid with a wad of tenners, she found it impossible not to think how awful it was that Mrs Fraser wasn't around anymore. She was the teacher who'd helped Emily when she most needed it. Year Six in Alderton Primary could have been a nightmare, but Mrs Fraser had convinced her she could rise above her family problems. How good was that?

How could somebody like that have been killed? DC Travis' question about Mrs Fraser's love life got her thinking. It was hard to imagine that side of her former teacher's life. She remembered introducing her to Mark in the pub last year some time. He had said she was good-looking. Good-looking, nice personality, no husband on the scene, you'd expect her to be involved with some guy or other.

As she listened with as much patience as she could muster to a woman complaining about her poor mobile reception in Castlebridge, Emily thought about the police's angle. They must have thought Dawn Fraser's love life was important; otherwise why ask about it? Who did kill her? The boyfriend or husband was always the prime suspect. In other words, the person who was supposed to love her. How did that work?

On her way to M&S for a lunchtime sandwich, Emily tried to forget about Dawn Fraser and consider her future. Decisions, decisions. At least she knew she had her whole life in front of her. That was what anybody over the age of thirty-five constantly told her. As though the blindingly obvious were some newly discovered philosophical gem. That was the trouble with older people: they thought they knew it all.

Emily had spent countless hours longing to get away from Alderton. She had lived in the village all her life and had no wish to die there. Shouldn't she be really happy at the prospect of university in the autumn? Studying law at University College, London, how cool was that? Annoyingly, though, she was now getting cold feet about it. Would all those southern sophisticates look down on a girl from the north east? Maybe she was being unfair on

Lovendale. It was a beautiful place. Some really bad stuff had happened to her there but it wasn't Alderton's fault.

She wanted to get away from Mum, that went without saying. Dad was a different matter. She'd be happier about leaving if she weren't worried about abandoning him. Now, a year after A levels, it was time to put up or shut up. If she didn't make her mind up soon, it would be too late. She'd would be stuck in the Avanatta shop, selling mobile phones if she didn't watch out.

Still she couldn't stop thinking about last Friday, probably Dawn's last day on earth. Emily had had her final therapy session with Bev in the familiar room above the Northern Bank in Front Street. What had eight weeks of heart-searching achieved? Well, she had got things a bit more in perspective. And she could start to plan her next move. Bev had said Emily had to face up to harsh reality at a much younger age than most people. Harsh reality meant her mother was a self-centred tosser but Bev couldn't say so. Non-directive counselling she called it.

Until half-way through the sessions the mere mention of Mum's name would trigger the barely controlled rage that simmered beneath the surface. Emily would launch into a tirade about her at such times, and had felt so liberated when Bev said it was OK to feel angry. She had learnt to take her anger to the sessions so it didn't get in the way the rest of the time. On the whole that had worked: she hadn't felt like murdering anybody for days now.

* * *

A couple of hours later, Tiffany Booth came into the shop.

"Hiya, Emily," she said, loud enough for the whole of Front Street to hear her.

"Hi. What can I help you with?"

"I'm after an iPhone 8."

Emily gave her the spiel she had learned off by heart, explained the unique features, went through special offers only available from Avanatta. Her eyes opened wide when Tiffany chose the most expensive option.

"Wondering where I get my money from, are you? All I can say is I've got little Harry to thank for this."

CHAPTER NINE

Mark slowed the Toyota Supra at the traffic lights on the Loventon ring road near the Empire Theatre. He still couldn't get his head round what had happened to Dawn. He thought back to that Friday night in the Bricklayers a few days before Christmas. Emily had introduced him to Dawn, who'd been having a drink with a woman she worked with. The tight white jumper and jeans did something for her. They did something for Mark as well.

She wasn't legless or anything, but she'd had a few. It was obvious to Mark's practised eye she was coming on to him. As she was leaving with her friend, she whispered an invitation to call round the next morning for an early Christmas present.

Emily always called her Mrs Fraser, with her being a teacher. Well, she'd taught him a thing or two all right. He grinned at the memory. Images of his and Dawn's bodies twisting into impossible positions flooded into his head. How he would love the chance to be with her one more time. Not going to happen. Get over it. He'd always had a thing about older women, which made it strange he was going out with Emily.

In a funny sort of way, though, Emily *was* an older woman. She didn't look old, nothing like that, but she was more… what would you call it? He couldn't think of the right word, but it was like she had everything worked out. The way she talked and everything, the books she'd read and all the exams she'd passed. She even had her appearance under control, her fair hair always neat and tidy.

And she wore glasses. As well as being a bit of a turn on for him, that gave her a bit of class. It did his image no harm to be seen with somebody like her. Made people take him more seriously. Good for his career. She was the sort of girl he should marry, someone from a different background.

He sometimes wondered about Emily. What was she all about? She never said much about her family, just the odd hint, but Mark had a feeling something wasn't right. Her parents were divorced, he thought, not together anyway. Her mam was on the council and worked for an accountancy firm in Loventon. Emily didn't have much time for her mother, dismissing her as 'a bit of a weirdo'. She even blamed her mam for her bad eyesight.

Her dad seemed OK on the two or three occasions Mark had met him. Not as posh as his daughter but not one of the lads. He didn't drink much for a kick-off. He was into cricket as well; now that was hard to fathom. Well off though. His house was worth a bit and he owned two holiday flats in Alderton.

That was the sort of thing Mark aspired to. For a lad from the Moor Park estate he hadn't done bad so far, but he had to do better. He usually kept his background quiet, people could be sniffy about it. Having a brother in the nick and a sister on probation wouldn't impress many people.

Emily didn't seem to mind, though; she said her grandma and granddad had started life on Moor Park and they'd done OK. Well, the same could be said about him.

He'd be an Avanatta shop manager before long. Then climb the ladder. A picture flashed into his mind of him and Emily in ten years' time. They'd have a couple of kids, a five-bedroom detached in Alderton, a bit of land. Top of the range Land Rover. He'd certainly make a better job of being a father than his own dad, wherever he was.

What had that copper wanted with Emily? Was it about Dawn? Luckily, he had an excuse for getting out of the way. Had some nosy villager seen him driving through Alderton last Friday? That would really set the cat among the pigeons, put him right in the frame. He didn't want the cops questioning him, maybe finding out about his bit on the side. It was vital Emily knew nothing about it for one thing. He could do without too many complications in his life.

He left the town centre, looking forward to seeing Siobhain, the Avanatta manager at Castlebridge. The way she looked at him sometimes, it could drive a guy mad. Somebody had told him Siobhain was forty-five. That hadn't put him off, why should it? He would definitely make a move one of these days. Why not today?

He got to the Castlebridge branch only to find out it was Siobhain's day off. While he was waiting for a spotty lad to bring the phones he'd come to collect, Mark looked round the shop. He thought about the rumours going around about redundancies. He'd even heard that one of the local branches was about to shut down. It wouldn't be Loventon if he had anything to do with it. Judging by the lack of customers, this place would be top of the list for closure. A voice to his left interrupted his musing.

"It's Mark Hanwell, isn't it?"

He turned to see a dark haired woman of about thirty. Jeans and T-shirt. Bag slung over her shoulder.

"That's right."

"Don't you remember me?"

He looked her over, trying to place her.

"I used to teach you," she explained.

It only took a second to think of the name.

"Miss Brent of course. Seeing you in a different context threw me for a second. How are you?"

"Fine. It must be six or seven years since you left sixth form college, Mark."

"Dropped out halfway through, you mean."

"You could have done well."

He shrugged.

"I couldn't hack it. I mean, I enjoyed English, I've always loved reading, but writing essays about novels and plays took all the enjoyment out of them."

"I sometimes think that myself."

"And the pseudo-intellectual geeks who spouted some garbage about symbolism and dramatic irony drove me half barmy."

"Me too. What do you do now?" she asked.

"Assistant manager in the Avanatta shop in Loventon. I had to come over here on business."

"Loventon? You'll know Emily Flint then."

"Yeah, I know Emily."

"Is she OK?"

"Yeah. Upset about one of her teachers being killed. Mrs Fraser, I think her name was."

"Dawn, yes, she was a good friend of mine. Dreadful, wasn't it?"

He nodded, having nothing to say. Miss Brent filled the conversational gap.

"It seems she died over the bank holiday weekend. I was meant to be going round to hers for a drink on the Friday, but I had to cancel. I didn't hear about her death for a few days. I was visiting friends in London. Actually Nadia, Emily's mother, was with me."

When Miss Brent left the shop, Mark thought about what she had said about knowing Dawn and Emily's mam. Did that mean Nadia knew Dawn as well? Mark only hoped Dawn hadn't let his name slip out during one of their social gatherings. Something else to worry about.

CHAPTER TEN

"I'm not sure this is a good idea, Kate," said Michelle the following Monday. "I've always been wary of the media."

Kate looked over to her friend and tried to reassure her.

"Isn't this journalist an old friend? Surely he won't give you a hard time."

Michelle glanced at her watch for the sixth time in the past five minutes.

"Yeah, he's OK Dale, from good farming stock, very down to earth. Maybe a bit more publicity will do some good. Everybody reads the Chronicle round here."

"The media has its uses," said Kate.

"Yes. I only hope he's on time. Clive's coming round to finalise the funeral arrangements later."

"It's so frustrating," Michelle went on after a pause, "the police are getting nowhere. I'm sure I read somewhere most murders are solved pretty quickly."

"Well, it's particularly difficult when somebody nice is killed. It can take time to find an obvious suspect."

Michelle's hand shook slightly as she tried to stop more tears from flowing.

"In Dawn's case it's even harder without a partner. He would have been the first person the police might suspect."

"Yes, but somebody killed her," said Michelle just as the front door bell rang.

*** * ***

Half an hour later the interview for the local paper was over. Dale Wilson, a tall guy of about forty, who looked as though a puff of wind would blow him over, had asked his questions efficiently but sympathetically.

"Thanks very much, Michelle. I know how hard it must be for you. Nice meeting you, Kate," said the reporter, getting up to go.

"Oh, Dale," said Michelle, "I meant to ask you, have the police spoken to you at all?"

"Why do you ask?"

"I heard you were near here on the day Dawn was murdered."

"How did you...? Listen, I can't talk about it."

Michelle looked hard at the journalist.

"I think you're gonna have to."

He sat down again, panic gripping him. He let out a loud sigh and finally spoke.

"I may as well tell you... the police gave me a grilling last night."

Kate exchanged a glance with Michelle.

"They found a text from me on Dawn's phone."

He opened his mouth to say more but thought better of it.

"Dale, you're not making any sense," said Michelle. "Why should a text lead to a grilling from the police."

He ran his hand across his chin.

"It wasn't just that. What you heard is true, Michelle. I was round Loven Terrace last Friday afternoon and somebody saw me."

"Right. Where were you going?"

"To see Dawn. I'd arranged to meet her here."

"Here?"

Michelle sounded affronted.

"Yeah, she said she had to be at her sister's house after school, why didn't I come and see her?"

"What?" said Michelle.

"Me and Dawn had been having a bit of a thing for a while. Nobody knew about it. She insisted on that."

"Dale, I can't believe this," said Michelle. "You and my sister were lovers and... was it serious?"

"Not to her it wasn't. I wanted it to be. You probably remember me and Dawn were an item when we were about sixteen. Well, I was in love with her even then. I thought she felt the same, but..."

He shrugged.

"She met Ed and that was it. I wasn't surprised when he walked out, I told her from the start he wasn't right for her. But at least it gave me a chance, or so I thought. Trouble was I never had the nerve to do anything about it."

"Then how did it start?" asked Kate.

"Dawn called me some time in March. Right out of the blue. She told me she had a new role in the school, something to do with public relations. The idea was to get success stories about Alderton Academy in the media."

"And?"

"I went to see her at home and we ended up in bed together. It was wonderful. Far removed from teenage fumbling – when we first went out together we never actually, you know..."

A faraway look came into his eyes. Michelle found her voice.

"Dale, for Christ's sake. Too much information. Just tell me how you managed to keep this quiet."

Dale was looking pole-axed by now, but he managed to reply.

"We only met on and off. There was always a story I put in the paper as a kind of pretext for us meeting. We never went out on a proper date or anything."

"Right," said Kate, "on the day Dawn died, what happened when you saw her?"

Kate realised she was acting like a copper but what the hell?

"That's just it. I didn't get to see her. I turned up as arranged about five o'clock. I called round here but got no answer. Went to Dawn's place, nobody in. I tried texting her; called her mobile and landline; no answer."

He closed his eyes momentarily, swearing under his breath. Kate and Michelle looked at one another in silent bewilderment for a while. Kate went on with her questioning.

"You told the police all this, I take it?"

"Yeah."

"When you were in Alderton that day, did you see anyone?"

He looked relieved to have moved away from his relationship with Dawn.

"I remember the 37 to Loventon was just leaving. There were people about but I didn't take much notice. Paddy McCann was walking ahead of me, I don't think he saw me."

"Who's he?" asked Kate. "I've heard the name but I can't remember in what context."

"You'll soon get to know Paddy," said Michelle. "He lives in the village. Big noise in the Labour Party, leader of the council, wealthy businessman. Influential, I guess you'd call him."

"What's he like?" asked Kate.

"Hail-fellow-well-met type. His second wife's half his age, but that doesn't stop him chasing other women."

"I play golf with him occasionally in the hope of getting a story," said Dale, "but I never get anywhere. He's a typical politician, takes a long time to say not very much."

"Would he have known Dawn?"

"Yes, I think so. They weren't friends or anything but Paddy liked to think he knew everybody. Dawn was well-known in the village because she was involved in so many things."

"Did you tell the police you'd seen Mr McCann?"

"Yes. That detective sergeant was a bit snotty about it. He said, 'We are aware that Mr McCann was in the vicinity; he contacted us after we had appealed for information. It's a pity you didn't do the same.'"

"Oh, dear," said Michelle.

"It looks bad that I didn't come forward before they got in touch with me. I should have been more proactive. I'm a suspect, that much is obvious."

"Surely not, Dale," said Michelle.

"It's ridiculous, I loved Dawn, I would never have hurt her."

He looked pleadingly at Michelle.

"You know what?" he continued. "They even hinted I was some sort of sicko, killing people then writing about it in the paper. Trying to make a name for myself."

* * *

After the panicky reporter had gone, Michelle went straight to the loo, giving Kate a chance to think. She knew Dawn Fraser was too good to be true. Right from the start she had never believed in the perfect teacher who lived the life of a nun. What other secrets had she been keeping? Once again Kate was in detective mode, thinking about the murder. The trouble was she had very little to go on.

"Well, that's a turn up, isn't it?" asked Michelle when she got back.

"Yes. Do you know Dale well?"

"Pretty well. He thinks he's a suspect. That can't be right."

"The police will be looking at him, I'm afraid."

"But he wouldn't have had any reason to kill Dawn. Surely he would have wanted Dawn to stay alive."

Kate wasn't so sure.

"Unless she dumped him."

"Dale wouldn't hurt a fly," said Michelle with some force. "I've known him all my life practically."

"Anyway, I'll just nip to the shop before Clive gets here," said Kate, "I won't be long."

On her way, Kate thought again about Dale Wilson. Michelle wanted to think the best about her friend and she was reluctant to disabuse her. A career spent witnessing the worst of human nature close-up had frequently led her to think the unthinkable, but Michelle would not want to do that in relation to someone she knew. Dale might come across as Mr Nice Guy but who knew what he was capable of? She reminded herself that Rolf Harris took part in an NSPCC video about the dangers of sexual abuse. Now look at him.

* * *

"So how do you like life in Lovendale, Kate?" asked Clive Wheatley, biting into a ginger biscuit and sipping his tea.

Now that the funeral arrangements had been made, it was time for idle chit chat.

"It's rather difficult to say. It's very beautiful and the people are nice, but it's been one shock after another since I got here."

"Kate ended up in hospital within half an hour of her arrival," said Michelle.

"Oh, dear."

Clive slipped on an expression of grave concern like a mask. Kate felt compelled to tell the vicar about the row between Rebecca and Tiffany and her collision with the freezer.

"Are you all right?"

"Fine."

Sipping more tea, he looked thoughtfully at Kate.

"With the best will in the world, it's hard not to think that Tiffany Booth is a little unstable."

"That's the nearest Clive gets to slagging anyone off," said Michelle.

"I suppose slagging off isn't included in a vicar's job description", said Kate.

Michelle explained.

"Clive meant to say Tiffany flies off the handle at the least provocation, will shag anything that moves and can be a devious so and so. Isn't that right, Clive?"

He smiled conspiratorially.

"Perhaps I would not have used those exact words but there could be an element of truth in what you say."

* * *

Later that day, Kate went into the back yard, convinced there was more to discover about what happened to Dawn. She wasn't of course investigating the murder, she wouldn't dream of it. How would she have liked it if some ex DI had stuck her nose into one of her cases? On the other hand, a little research would help her to answer any questions Michelle might have. Her experience told her speculation was pointless without something concrete. Hence her examination of the scene of the crime.

Michelle's yard was identical to Sam's but had a neglected look. It was hard to imagine anybody sitting out here on a summer's day with a glass of chilled Pinot Grigio. It needed a picnic table like Sam's and a few of his pots and hanging baskets. But she wasn't here to assess the beauty of the place.

She walked slowly on the uneven paving stones, similar to the ones found in any street, trying to get a feel for the place. None of the houses in this terrace had a garden. The residents presumably made what they could of the tiny space they'd been allotted. Not Michelle though. She was so organised about her career, yet everything else was left to sort itself out.

Kate begged her surroundings to speak to her. A brick wall to the left formed a boundary with the house next door. At the end of the yard, the wooden shed was on its last legs. If anybody were looking for the ideal murder site, this was as good as any. It was quiet and very few people passed along the lane at the back of the houses; the wall at the end was high enough for the killer not to be overlooked. She walked to the wooden outside door, about five feet high and never locked. Anyone could come and go without much chance of being seen or heard.

How did it happen? The body had been moved, that much was certain. Dawn must have been killed in the house, but what happened immediately after the murder? The killer would have had to carry or drag the body across the yard. Which was it? Did it matter?

It would take a degree of strength to heave a dead body across one's shoulder. There were strong women but the carrier would most likely be a man. That assumed it would be easier to drag a corpse. One wouldn't have to take the full weight but it would still be quite an effort. Unlike Kate, DS Penrose would have forensic evidence that pointed him in the right direction.

The murderer probably entered by the back door to minimise the chance of being caught. So he or she would have left in the same way. Most murder victims were killed by somebody they knew. Only helpful up to a point, thought Kate. Everybody knew Mrs Fraser, though nobody seemed to know her well, not even Dale.

Another thing had been bothering Kate: why was Dawn in motorbike gear when her body was discovered? Where could she have been going? She wasn't due to go away until the next day.

Kate opened the shed door, switched the light on and went in. Not many clues there, she said to herself. Apart from a table with three legs propped precariously against the left hand wall, a cardboard box full of nails and screws and a wheelie bin, the place was empty. Sergeant Penrose and his team would have taken away anything remotely useful. For the sake of thoroughness Kate walked over to the far corner where Dawn had been found. She wondered how the wooden joist held Dawn's weight. She was small and light but even so.

Kate was supposed to be in Alderton to make a break with the past, to sort her life out. She had given up her job to be here. Why then was she doing detective work in her friend's back yard? Did that mean she missed the Met?

No. She was only doing the interesting bit now. She could never go back to manoeuvring her way round the management hierarchy, the long hours, the pressure to get results. What would she do instead? The ringing of the house phone allowed her to postpone consideration of that impossible question for a bit longer. She rushed indoors to answer it.

"Hello?"

"Is that Miss Thomas?"

It was a woman, local, young-sounding.

"No, I can take a message if you like. Who's calling?"

"It's Code and Godfrey – solicitors."

"Can I ask what it's in connection with?"

Silence on the end of the line for a few seconds.

"Well, it's a family matter. I can't say any more than that."

* * *

As soon as Kate passed on the message, Michelle sat in the living room and dialled the solicitor's number, while Kate went to make coffee. When she came back, Michelle was talking.

"You mean she had an appointment today?"

Kate listened with great interest.

"But why wait until now? She must have arranged this... yes, I see... well, of course you should tell the police, they're investigating a murder."

Michelle pursed her lips, gripping the arm of the settee.

"Confidentiality be blowed... if you don't ring them, I will and I expect you'll have a visit within the hour... good. Now you can tell me what the appointment was about."

Now Michelle moved the telephone from one ear to the other and drummed her fingers on the settee.

"Here's how it works: when you tell the police, they will tell me so they can get my reaction. So you may as well tell me now… What? Oh, I see. Thank you very much."

She ended the call and looked at Kate.

"Dawn made an appointment for half eleven this morning with Code and Godfrey. She was planning to start divorce proceedings on grounds of desertion and change her will, leaving everything to me."

CHAPTER ELEVEN

"Kate, this is Emily, my daughter," said Sam.

Emily shook hands with a woman in a charcoal grey linen trouser suit, standing next to Michelle in the porch of St Gregory's. Her brown hair was long, straight and shining with health. Kate had a kind of effortless style about her.

Even her dad looked quite distinguished in a dark suit, but here she was feeling too warm in a black skirt and jacket, the nearest things she had to funeral clothes. They made their way inside the church and took their seats at the back. Michelle went to the front to join the rest of her family.

Emily looked round the packed church. Could Dawn Fraser possibly have known everybody here? The local media was represented by Lita Bridge from the local TV news; a scruffy, old bloke from Radio Lovendale; and Dale Wilson, of course, he got everywhere. She recognised quite a few people she knew from school – they must have accounted for a large percentage of the congregation.

Taking in the rest of the mourners, she wondered if they were regular churchgoers. Or were they, like her, unwilling to go near a religious service except for occasions like this? As the ceremony went on, Emily thought of what Dad had said about all the people who were benefitting from Dawn's murder. Local media, undertakers, florists. Not to mention the Church of England. The vicar turned to face the assembled friends and family of the deceased.

"We are here to celebrate the life of Dawn Amber Fraser. Dawn was a much-loved and respected teacher. She was also a daughter and a sister. Her life was cut short in the most horrendous and seemingly pointless way. At a time like this, it is easy to lose one's faith in the almighty, to ask how a loving God can allow these things to happen. Such a response is understandable..."

Clive gave way to the head of Alderton Primary, Ian somebody, who recited all Mrs Fraser's virtues. Then Michelle climbed the pulpit steps. She spoke in a voice loaded with emotion. Unlike the previous two speakers she actually cared about Dawn. After a few seconds Emily recognised Psalm 23:

> *The Lord is my shepherd; I shall not want.*
>
> *He maketh me to lie down in green pastures: he leadeth me beside the still waters.*
>
> *He restoreth my soul: he leadeth me in the paths of righteousness for his name's sake.*
>
> *Yea, though I walk through the valley of the shadow of death, I will fear no evil...*

The language of the King James bible was so beautiful it was impossible not to be moved. For a few moments, Emily was carried away by the words, until the reality of what had happened came back to her. When the ceremony was over, everybody went outside into the sunshine. TV cameras on the grass in front of them tried to capture the scene.

"We're meant to go to Michelle's house now," said Sam, "She's organised..."

He stopped mid-sentence and turned to where a man in a shabby suit, tie askew, was running down the path towards the church. At the foot of the steps he stopped to get his breath back. Emily thought he looked familiar, but couldn't place him.

"Don't tell me I've missed it," he gasped.

"Ed! I don't believe it."

"Sam, how are you, mate?"

The latecomer, still taking in great lungfuls of air, thrust out his hand and shook Sam's, who began to introduce him to the others.

"Edward Fraser, Kate George. You remember Emily of course."

So that was who he was. Emily looked him up and down and wondered what Mrs Fraser could have seen in him. Ed looked much the same, though older, heavier, and scruffier. He'd never been a fine specimen of manhood, but at least he was well turned out when he was with Dawn. Couldn't he have made an effort to get here on time? And as he had not shown his face since he'd left, what was he doing here?

* * *

At Michelle's house, Kate made for the kitchen so she could help with the catering. Emily's Dad went off somewhere with Ed Fraser, leaving her closeted with Penny, whose black trousers and white top gave her an atypically formal air.

"Clive gave a very nice sermon," Emily said.

Penny looked incredulous.

"Was it?" she asked. "I gave up listening years ago. If you've heard one of Clive's homilies, Emily, you've heard them all."

"I've only heard one of course."

"You're lucky. Clive goes on as if they are works of art. He really thinks he's important because he..."

She let out a deep sigh of exasperation then went on moaning.

"What I do isn't important, of course. Unpaid work for the parish, looking after Jacob a mere bagatelle."

Emily smiled politely.

"Of course, Jacob's my total responsibility. Clive does none of his son's day-to-day care. Never changed a nappy in his life. And Jacob's so lovely, Emily, as you know. You'd think Clive would want to spend more time with him. He quoted something from the Bible to justify his attitude. He always turns to the good book when it suits him."

"Well..."

"I'm a full-time mother of course," Penny went on, "the adoption process took so long I thought we'd never have a real live baby. Now that we have, I'm going to enjoy the experience. I had to sacrifice my career, but it was well worth it."

"You were one of the top managers at Avanatta, weren't you?"

Penny nodded.

"Yes, I fancied myself as a pretty ruthless operator in those days. I was heading for the top and nobody was going to stop me. I have different priorities now."

"I suppose you're grateful Jacob's too young to understand about Dawn dying?" said Emily.

"Oh, yes."

"Have you got over the shock of finding the body?"

"I wouldn't say I'd got over it exactly. I have flashbacks, you know? And the police are constantly coming round, 'just in case you've remembered anything else, Penny.' Not helpful as I'm sure you understand."

"Oh, yes."

"It's not as if I'm a trained police officer like Kate. I have no idea what to look out for, do I? If I've told them once, I've told them a thousand times, I can't help them."

When she finally got away from Penny, Emily considered what she'd said about not being able to help the police. It struck Emily then that the detectives looking into the death of Dawn Fraser must have come up against one major stumbling block: anybody who might have seen the murderer wasn't at home.

CHAPTER TWELVE

"Well, Sam, I suppose you're surprised to see me," said Edward Fraser.

"You could say that," I replied. "Are you gonna tell me where you've been for the past two years or what?"

Ed had suggested we go into Michelle's yard so he could smoke. I was reluctant to go near the scene of Dawn's death but Ed's craving for nicotine took precedence over other considerations. After five minutes of bringing him up to date with my life, it took a direct question for Ed to even begin to explain himself.

"Sheffield."

Ed swigged at a can of Fosters. He'd got stuck into the booze moments after setting foot in Michelle's house. I shouldn't do it, but I'd never been able to kick the habit of noticing how much people drank. I never commented though. I wasn't that daft.

"Follow up question: what were you doing there?"

He took a drag from his cigarette.

"I was manager of Next in the Meadowhall Centre."

I presumed Meadowhall was a soulless collection of shops somewhere in South Yorkshire.

"What? You left Dawn to do the same job you were doing in Loventon?"

I'd never been to Sheffield and no doubt it was a nice enough place, but I'd expected him to have gone to, say, New York, St Tropez or Barbados. Somewhere glamorous anyway.

"Not really. It was... well, there's more to it than that, Sam."

I waited, my impatience growing by the minute. He sucked more smoke into his lungs.

"I'd done loads of applications before I was offered the Sheffield job. I was chuffed to bits. It was a big promotion, more money, a change for God's sake."

"Right."

"When I told Dawn about it, I was expecting her to be as excited as me."

He began to pace about, blowing smoke through his teeth.

"But she wasn't?"

He stopped pacing and pointed at me.

"Got it in one. It was too far away. Lovendale was her home, she could never leave, what about her job?"

He looked down at the ground then back at Sam.

"I told her she could get a job in Sheffield. If she didn't fancy teaching in the city, there was the Peak District on the doorstep. A nice village school would be ideal."

He poured more lager down his throat.

"I couldn't persuade her. I gave it a week and it was still no good. I said I'd phone and tell them I couldn't take the job."

"But..."

"I lied, OK? Not right, I know and maybe I chickened out, wasn't straight with her, whatever..."

Silence fell as Ed looked down at the paving stones.

"I just... God, Sam, I couldn't stand the thought of being stuck round here for the rest of my life."

No doubt it was much more exciting to be stuck in Sheffield. Being stuck, what was that all about? We were all stuck; didn't it depend on how you defined these things? Being stuck is a state of mind, I said to myself. Ed, unaware of my profound insights, went on with his story.

"I just couldn't face telling her, so I decided to go without her. One day after work I got in my car and drove off. I told Dawn I'd been sent on a training course. I took out half the money from our savings account and as many clothes as would fit in one suitcase."

He must have been thinking about leaving Dawn for a canny while. Had he just been looking for an excuse?

"I stayed in the Ibis hotel and phoned Dawn the next morning after breakfast. Said I was going travelling, there was no point in looking for me."

"I can't believe it, it's just..."

Words failed me. I'd seen a documentary once about people who go missing. I could never imagine knowing anybody like that. Then I'd never thought Nadia would leave me. Or that somebody would be murdered two doors away. These things happened every day. They had to happen somewhere.

"I got a flat in Hillsborough and tried to make a new life for myself. I've been there ever since."

For some reason, the idea that Ed had been in Hillsborough, a place I'd only ever thought about in relation to Sheffield Wednesday football team and the disaster in the late eighties, struck me as bizarre.

"Are you still at Next?"

He shook his head.

"I got made redundant about six weeks ago."

More lager went down the hatch. He shook the empty can, then crushed it.

"I got a good pay out but I can't see it lasting too long if I don't get another job soon."

"So are you, you know, with anybody?"

He shrugged.

"Not really."

Whatever that meant. He still hadn't explained what had brought him here today.

"How did you find out Dawn had died?"

"Lovendale Chronicle online. I have a look at it from time to time. Curiosity, I guess. When I read about Dawn, it was a hell of a shock, I can tell you. I couldn't believe it."

"Nor could anybody, Ed."

He nodded, passing the can from one hand to the other.

"Then when I heard she'd been murdered, I knew I had to go to the funeral. To, you know, say goodbye properly, like."

"Have you not been back at all since you left?"

He shook his head.

"No need to until now. My mam and dad went to live in Spain ages ago and my brother's been in Chesterfield for years."

"What about your mates?"

He shrugged, taking another drag on his fag.

"If I came back, I would have seen Dawn. She would have sucked me back in. You don't know what she was like."

I was getting impatient at Ed's whingeing about his oppressive marriage.

"Oh, come on, mate, I don't buy this idea of Dawn, of all people, being some sort of a control freak."

He shook his head.

"That's not what I'm saying, Sam. She wasn't horrible; it was more subtle than that."

Too subtle for me anyway. Did Ed feel he ought to follow in the footsteps of his family and get away from Lovendale? Was that it? Thinking back, I was surprised he had been well-organised enough to get as far as Sheffield. We always used to say Ed would be late for his own funeral. Late for your wife's, that was near enough.

I looked at my old friend, wondering what was really behind his arrival here today. Since I had last seen him, my life had changed. I had changed. All that had happened since had made me look at people with a more jaundiced eye. I no longer saw Ed Fraser, great bloke, but a stranger who could walk out on his wife without being honest with her. What was he up to?

I was about to leave, when a man of about seventy came out of the house to join us. He lit a cigar with a gold lighter and smiled uncertainly.

"May I join you?"

"Sure," I said.

"I'm Quentin Diplock, by the way."

It was only then I noticed his dog collar.

"Sam Flint. This is Ed Fraser, Dawn's husband."

The two men nodded at one another.

"May I offer my sincere condolences," said the bishop.

"Thanks."

Ed opened another can of lager and took a swig.

"She was a good, Christian woman," added Quentin.

Ed scowled.

"That was a bone of contention between us and all. One of many. The last thing I wanted was to be married to a God-botherer."

Diplock puffed on his cigar.

"I hear you're retiring," I said, anxious to avoid an argument.

The last thing we needed at Dawn's funeral was her husband locking horns with the Bishop of Lovendale about religion. It caused enough trouble as it was.

"Yes. A relief in many ways."

I could never imagine retiring. Getting paid for something I liked doing was good enough for me. Anyway, what else would I do?

"Have you got any thoughts about your successor?"

"As a matter of fact, I have," he replied. "Of course, I can't say anything. They'd probably defrock me."

"We can't have that."

Ed had been observing the conversation without much interest. Now he chipped in.

"Why not a local lad? Or a local woman. There's that lass who's the vicar in Castlebridge."

I couldn't care less who the next bishop would be so I decided to leave. As I got back inside the house, Clive waylaid me. Another God-botherer, I thought.

"Sam, glad you could make it," he said, thrusting out his hand for all the world as if he were a host welcoming guests to a party. The glass of white wine in his hand added to the feeling of celebration.

"Least I could do. A sad day. Michelle must be finding it hard."

Clive nodded, trying to look wise and understanding.

"Oh, indeed. And just as she's wanting to grieve, there are all the practical details to sort out."

"Yeah."

"The funeral of course, all Dawn's belongings, the will..."

"She made a will then?"

He drank more wine.

"Oh, yes, when she and Ed got married. He inherited everything."

Was that why Ed was here? To make sure he got what was his? The house alone could fetch two hundred grand. Handy for someone who'd just lost his job.

"I didn't realise that. On top of all that there's a criminal investigation."

Clive nodded.

"Yes. Now that Ed has turned up, I presume the police will want to see him. They've talked to everybody else. Pity none of us could help them."

Clive smiled sadly. At that point, Kate joined us. I introduced her to Clive.

"A lovely service," she said.

"Thank you," murmured Clive, "I hope it provided some comfort."

After a bit more chat, Clive left us.

"I can never make him out," I said.

"Mmm, I know what you mean. He must have had to develop a sort of persona. I mean, vicars always seem to have this very caring voice..."

She changed her intonation for the last few words to illustrate her point. I chuckled at this. I'd never thought of it that way before but she was spot on.

"The only time I've seen Clive let the mask slip," I said, "was when he threw that punch at Paddy McCann."

"Oh, yes, I remember you telling me. I suppose it proves he's human. Not that I'm advocating going around thumping people."

"I'm glad to hear it. You must have got involved in some fights when you were in the Met."

She smiled.

"Fewer than you might think. If anybody got out of hand, my judo came in handy."

I smiled back.

"Judo, eh? I'll have to remember that."

"You need to keep on the right side of me."

That would be nice, I thought.

CHAPTER THIRTEEN

"She'll be sadly missed, Kate," said Ian Hood, a short, plump man with sparse grey hair. "The school isn't the same without her."

Kate had been introduced to the Alderton Academy head teacher by Michelle, who had then excused herself, saying she needed fresh air.

"I'm just beginning to realise how much Dawn was admired," said Kate.

"She was a natural teacher, I could never picture her doing any other job. You can't say that about everyone."

Ian was around fifty but had the air of a precocious schoolboy who rather fancied himself.

"The way she died makes it worse in a way, the police having to be involved and everything."

"Of course. They paid a couple of visits to the school actually."

"I expect they found it really useful to talk to you, Ian."

He shrugged modestly.

"I like to think so. I didn't know a lot about Dawn's life outside school. She was friendly enough, don't get me wrong, but she kept herself to herself."

He had a ponderous way of talking as though every word was worth its weight in gold.

"I'm sort of getting that impression. You seem an observant kind of guy, though, I'm sure you noticed something of value to DS Penrose."

Ian Hood swelled with pride.

"Well, there were a couple of things I passed on..."

Kate smiled sweetly and waited.

"One lunchtime a few days before Dawn died, she was alone in her classroom talking on her phone. I overheard just a few words as I walked by, something like, 'you realise what you're doing constitutes stalking?'"

"Oh, my God."

"It disturbed me at the time and of course it came back to me when the police came to see me yesterday."

"That puts a new light on things all right."

"That's what I thought."

"She didn't talk to you about this stalker, give you any clue as to who it was?"

"I only wish she had."

"What was the second thing you passed on?"

"Yes, that was odd too in a different way," said Ian. "She saw someone going into the Market Tavern in Loventon and for a moment thought it was her husband..."

"When was this?"

"She told me about it on the day she died, so I reckon it was the day before."

The headteacher left shortly after this. Sam's daughter came into the room and walked over to Kate.

"Hi," said Emily.

"Hi. You OK? I understand Dawn used to teach you."

"Yeah, she helped me a lot. I only hope it's all resolved quickly for Michelle's sake."

"Of course."

"I don't suppose the police have confided in you, have they, Kate? You were in CID, weren't you?"

"Yes, but that doesn't give me any special privileges, I'm afraid. I'm treated the same as everybody else."

"Right. Does that mean you were interviewed and stuff?"

"Yes. DS Penrose asked the sort of questions I've asked countless times."

"I was interviewed by a detective constable," said Emily. "She seemed to think I might have been the last person to see Mrs Fraser alive. A bit spooky, that."

"Yes, isn't it? When was this?"

"Around half four on the day she died."

Emily explained about talking to Dawn at the bus stop. They talked for a few more minutes before Emily said she'd better be going.

"I'll just find Michelle and say goodbye. Nice meeting you."

* * *

As Emily departed, Kate thought what a nice girl she was. Was she really the last person to see the murdered woman alive? Apart from the murderer of course. That would make it easier to work out when Dawn Fraser was killed, but gave no clue about the perpetrator. Dawn had been having a dalliance with her old flame, Dale Wilson; there was the possibility of a stalker; she might have seen Edward Fraser the day before she died. Things were getting complicated.

* * *

After the funeral, Kate changed into jeans and trainers and walked across Loven bridge, away from the village, then followed the footpath through Alderton Woods. The barking of a dog in the distance, the wind through the trees and the rippling of Crow Beck accompanied her. As she climbed a wooden stile, the sight of a heron motionless in the water gave her a moment of wonder.

Well, that was something she had never seen before. Perhaps she was turning into a country bumpkin.

With each step, though not actually investigating the murder, she tried to think through logically what she knew. Were there any patterns? Was it possible to make sense of it all? Dawn must have been killed in Michelle's house. The murderer must have put the body in the shed to delay its discovery. Did he or she know Dawn had arranged to go away the next day and wouldn't be missed for a while?

Dawn was at school all day on the Friday when she was probably killed; Emily Flint saw her at around half past four. She was most likely murdered soon after getting to Michelle's house. She was only there to get the house ready for Kate to move in so wouldn't have been planning to stay long.

None of the neighbours were around at the relevant time. Penny was visiting her mother, her husband was away on a retreat or something. Michelle was in Edinburgh, Sam was on a walk. Emily got the bus into town shortly after seeing Dawn. The police must have been hoping one of them would have noticed something. Had the murderer planned everything to happen at a time when there'd probably be no witnesses?

* * *

"I'm thinking of inviting Ed round, what do you think?" asked Michelle the next morning over breakfast.

Kate ate a spoonful of cornflakes and considered the question.

"Up to you."

Michelle sipped her coffee.

"I mean, I'm still angry with him for abandoning my sister but I feel it would help me to talk about Dawn with somebody who knew her."

"That makes sense," said Kate.

"Would you be there with me?"

"Sure. You do realise Ed's a suspect? The husband always is."

Michelle nodded sadly.

* * *

"Yeah, she was a great girl," said Edward Fraser the following evening.

In the past hour, he had got through three cans of Guinness with a kind of obsessive determination. Now he opened a fourth.

"Dawn told me not long ago she thought she'd seen you recently," said Kate.

Ed stopped mid-swallow and put his can down on the table in front of him.

"Seen me?"

The surprise in his voice sounded genuine.

"Yes, going into the Market Tavern in Loventon one day."

He swigged more Guinness.

"No way. Dawn's funeral was the first time I'd been back here for two years."

"Have the police been to see you at all, Ed?" asked Kate.

"Not yet. I've got an appointment to go to the station at half two tomorrow. Purely routine, they said."

"Yes," agreed Michelle, "they have to be seen to be doing everything they can."

Ed finally got up to leave when the Guinness ran out.

"Before you go," Kate said, taking her phone from her handbag, "let me take a photo of you both."

Ed grinned.

"Why not?"

He put his arm round Michelle, his grin getting wider. Kate took three pictures, making sure one was of just Edward Fraser.

"I think I might have lunch at the Market Tavern tomorrow," she said to Michelle when Ed had gone.

Kate sat at the bar of the late nineteenth century pub, holding a menu. She'd taken the bus to Loventon with all the village pensioners and now, taking her first sip of Shiraz, she recalled her walk across the cobbled market square, the trendy bistro next to the pub, with the old market hall beyond that. Suitably impressed by the Victorian town, she felt rather shamefaced at the stereotypical view of the north she had brought with her.

"Seems to be a popular place, this," she said to the young barmaid.

"Oh, yes, rushed off our feet Friday lunchtime. You never been here before?"

"No, I've just moved into the area. It's a lovely town."

"Yeah, it's OK is Luvvo. Lived here all my life. Wouldn't want to move."

Kate smiled.

"A friend of mine recommended this place. Edward Fraser. Ed. Do you know him?"

"Doesn't ring a bell."

Kate took out her mobile and quickly found what she wanted.

"He lives in Sheffield now, but this used to be his local. In fact, he was in here a week or so ago. This is him here."

She held out the phone and pointed to the picture of Ed.

"Oh, I remember him. Hard to forget."

Kate perked up at this.

"Oh, really? Why was that?"

"Well, he was in a right state. You should have seen the amount he put down his throat. Rick refused to serve him in the end."

Ah, that would stick in someone's mind.

"He could hardly stand and he was being really, like, loud and that. Trying to chat me up. Gross."

"When was this?"

"Mmm, let me think now. End of May? Round about then anyway. It was the week the good weather started. Now, are you ready to order?"

Kate decided on lasagne and went to a corner table. She took a paperback from her rucksack and while reading, considered what she had discovered. Dawn did see her husband. Did it mean anything? It wouldn't be acceptable as evidence but who cared? She could forget the rules now. The most important question was: why did Edward Fraser lie about being in this pub?

* * *

Kate got back in time to see Sergeant Penrose driving away from Michelle's house. She found her friend in the living room with a large white wine in her hand, deep in thought.

"You OK?" she asked.

"Not sure," Michelle shrugged.

Kate sat down and waited.

"The police have just been. They have traced three men Dawn met and spent the night with while on her travels. One in Brighton, one in Worcester, one in Louth in Lincolnshire."

"Gosh."

Michelle took another mouthful of wine.

"They're just the ones who are known about. She seems to have been shagging her way round the country."

"A novel mode of transport," said Kate, "I only hope she enjoyed it."

They laughed together for the first time since Dawn had died.

"So do I."

Michelle shook her head gently from side to side.

"You know, Kate, I don't think I knew my sister at all."

CHAPTER FOURTEEN

As Emily walked along the footpath that ran parallel to the Loventon to Alderton road, she heard footsteps quite a way behind her. With Mrs Fraser being killed so close to home, it made sense to be a bit cautious. It must be nearly a month ago now but she couldn't get it out of her mind. The police seemed no nearer to an arrest, so the murderer was still out there somewhere. She felt inside her handbag and gripped the rape alarm. One press on that and there'd be a noise to wake up all the wildlife for miles around.

She was nearly halfway home now. Bird song, sporadic rustling in the undergrowth and the occasional hum of traffic had been the only sounds, until the footsteps. It was unusual for anybody else to be on the path at this time. She had got used to having it to herself.

She pressed on. The route was comfortably familiar by now. When she had started with Avanatta she'd decided bus into town in the morning and back home on foot was the way to go. The rhythm of movement relaxed her, giving her time and space to process all the stuff that was doing her head in.

Her dad had got her into walking when she was about ten. Getting out in the open did both of them good.

Around then mum was giving them a particularly hard time. Not that she had ever been easy. As well as the therapeutic aspect, walking was just good fun. Last year after A levels she'd done the Lovendale Way with a few friends. What a buzz that was. The footsteps were getting nearer now. Just one person, she reckoned.

To take her mind off the footsteps, she began to think of the little incidents that made up the working day. Selling mobile phones wasn't the most exciting job in the world but right from the start she had liked the idea of getting out of the house and going to work. The money came in handy and it helped her forget stuff she didn't want to think about. It gave her a new focus after the exams were over. Routine had always been her friend. It helped keep her sane in the bad times. Observing her mother's behaviour over the years had given her a terror of losing control.

She thought about her dad and hoped he hadn't been on his own all day. If only he could find himself a girlfriend. Everybody needed someone in their life. Having a boyfriend made Emily feel normal. Mark was a good laugh, everybody said so. Beneath the joking he was serious about her, she could tell. Too serious, dropping hints about getting engaged. She either didn't respond or pretended to misunderstand.

She knew she wasn't in love with him. She was usually pleased to see him but her heart didn't sing at the sight of him. Poor Mark, to be damned with such faint praise. Maybe it wasn't Mark, Emily might just not be ready for settling down. When – if – she went to uni, she might leave Mark to carve out a career for himself at Avanatta. He had a way with him so he'd soon find somebody else, but would she?

Where the path rose slightly above the road, a tractor trundled along, passing a sign saying 'Alderton 1 mile'. She walked more slowly to admire the landscape to the west. It was strange to think it had been scooped out by a glacier millions of years ago. The Lovendale Hills rolled into the distance, melting into one another like lovers.

The steep sides of the dale gave it an intimate, self-contained feel as though the rest of the world didn't exist. But it did exist, just over the horizon. Would Emily go out and explore it or stay here forever, become a shop manager, marry Mark because that was what people did? Maybe there was a tide in the affairs of women, which, taken at the flood, led on to fortune. With that thought to inspire her, she speeded up again. The footsteps followed her, not too far away now.

Emily's mind took her back to when she was a speccy, spotty fourteen year old, and one of the conservation volunteers who had laid this three mile footpath from Loventon to Alderton. At the time she'd enjoyed a rare period of happiness. Mum had been in the middle of one of her infrequent and short-lived good spells, showing how devoted she was by preparing her daughter's packed lunch every day. At the time, Emily thought it would last forever, that finally her troubles were behind her.

She was more realistic now and had to face the question, what should she do about Mum? The stand-off between them couldn't go on. Apart from anything else, it was upsetting Dad. Sighing, she realised it was up to her to sort it out. It was like she was the grown up, the one who had to see things clearly. Maybe now was the time. She had got this far in her reasoning when the footsteps caught up with her.

"Hello, Emily," said a voice she recognised, "Nice evening."

Oh, no, not him, she said under her breath.

"Oh, hi, Brian. Don't usually see you here."

Catching up with her, he moved so they were side by side, forcing her to edge away from him as far as she could. Slimy creep, she muttered inaudibly.

"No. Doctor's orders, take more exercise, he said. And it's good to take a break from the shop. Running your own business is no picnic in this day and age."

His prominent belly stuck out in front of him as if leading the way. The too-tight T-shirt, sweaty armpits and baggy shorts did nothing for him but then what would?

"I see they still haven't got anyone for Dawn Fraser's murder. Terrible business, isn't it?"

"Yes. She was a great teacher."

"So I heard. A great loss to the school and to her family too of course."

As she increased her pace, Brian struggled to keep up.

"Nothing but bad news lately," said Brian, "although I had a bit of good news a week or two back. The wife left me."

They walked on.

"How's Tiffany?" said Emily.

"Tiffany? What's she got to do with it?"

"Oh, I thought you and her were..."

"Well, we're not. If I never see her again it will be too soon. Tiffany Booth is pure evil. She finds things out about people and tries to, how can I put it, gain an advantage over them."

"Oh, yes?"

"Don't ever tell her anything you want to remain confidential. Soon the whole village will know about it, but in an exaggerated version."

"I'll remember that, Brian."

"Be sure you do. That Tiffany will upset one person too many one day. And she'll be sorry, you mark my words."

When, with a sigh of relief, Emily said goodbye to the appalling Brian and arrived at home, something happened to her. Now she knew for certain she couldn't stay here. She needed to change her life and had the opportunity to do so. She would go to university in October, see what the world had to offer. Meeting Brian had, against all the odds, done some good after all.

CHAPTER FIFTEEN

"Dad, I've made a decision at last," said Emily, "I'm definitely going to university in October."

"Great," I said, looking up from the local news on BBC One.

It was good and bad news: I knew it was right for her; at the same time, I didn't like to think about not seeing her for weeks at a time.

"And another thing," she went on. "I was wanting to have a word about Mum."

She'd obviously done some hard thinking on the walk home from work.

"Yeah?"

I made no further comment. It was a difficult subject, so the mere fact that Emily was mentioning her mother might mean we were on the verge of a breakthrough.

"I think it would be a good idea for me to start seeing her again."

She clenched her hands together tight enough to hurt.

"I mean, I know I said... well, if the three of us could get together occasionally. Not too often, I couldn't cope with that."

At least that would be a start. A bit like playing happy families, but I didn't have a better idea.

"That's fine with me," I said.

She unclenched her hands, tidied her fringe, took her glasses off and put them back on again.

"Could you call her for me?"

"Yeah, sure."

I got my phone out of my pocket and dialled.

"Hiya, Nadia," I said.

"Who's that?"

As if she didn't know.

"It's Sam."

"What do you want?"

Oh, no. There was a definite slur in her voice. As I was working out what to say, Emily's phone started to ring.

"Emily asked me to phone, she'd like to meet up with you..."

"Oh, would she? The little madam deigns to get in touch with her own mother. That's good of her. She took her time, didn't she? And why does she have to go through an interm, interm, intermediary?"

"Nadia, just..."

Meanwhile, Emily was talking on her mobile, "...oh, right... yeah, that should be OK... no bother, see you in a bit."

"Just nothing," snapped Nadia, "tell her she knows what she can do with herself and the same applies to you."

"Nadia, please think about what you're saying..."

No response. I was talking to myself.

"What did she say?" asked Emily.

How was I going to explain?

"Well, she..."

A look of determination on her face, Emily asked the question again.

"She's drunk."

Emily swallowed hard, shaking her head. I was reluctant to say any more. You were supposed to be honest with your kids, but there must be only so much honesty one person could take.

"She doesn't want to see me, does she?"

"I'm sure she didn't mean it, you know your mam's got a problem..."

Emily's snort of derision was more eloquent than words.

"Yeah, she's a pisshead...."

"Emily..."

"Still, I'm used to it. I've come second to alcohol, then it was her political career, followed by the so-called love of her life. Now it looks like it's all three of them."

I squeezed my hands into fists, wanting to shout, weep, punch something.

"Anyway, I haven't got time to bother about that right now," added Emily. "That was Penny on the phone. She needs me to babysit for an hour or so – she's going to some church meeting. Tiffany was supposed to be going round with Harry. The idea was she'd keep an eye on both kids while Penny was out."

"So what happened?"

Emily shrugged.

"Tiff didn't turn up. Never even called to say she couldn't make it. Anyway, I'd better get going."

"Are you sure you're OK? I could babysit if you like."

I didn't like the idea of her going out after that rejection from her mum.

"No way. Penny's paying me. I'll go straight to the Bricklayers from the vicarage."

Emily had dedicated herself to accumulating money for the past year. Her main job was in the Avanatta shop but she also acted as a sort of part-time secretary for me and cleaned my holiday flats. Add the odd bit of baby-sitting and an occasional shift at the pub and she'd soon be better off than me. She gave me a hug on the way out.

"Don't worry, Dad, I'll be fine. On reflection, I'm glad my so-called mother's back on the booze. With any luck she'll drink herself to death."

As she left, I turned back to the telly to see Alderton village green on the screen. In the background were the gates to Paddy McCann's place. Strange to see a familiar scene on telly; even stranger that Clive Wheatley was standing next to the glamorous *North East News* presenter, Lita Bridge. I turned the sound up.

> *"This idyllic village in the heart of Lovendale," she said, "is known for its beautiful scenery, country pubs and hillside walks but in recent weeks the killing of teacher, Dawn Fraser, has sent shockwaves through this tight-knit community. I have with me Clive Wheatley, vicar of St Gregory's in Alderton."*

She turned to Clive.

> *"This must be a difficult time for the local people."*

Clive nodded sagely.

> *"It certainly is, Lita."*

He spoke clearly, his voice throbbing with emotion.

> *"There has been grief, shock and, yes, a lot of anger directed at whoever was responsible for this outrage. Many of my parishioners are asking how such a thing can happen here."*

> *"What do you see as your role, Clive?"*

> *"The church can bring unity, pull everyone together and ensure life continues as it has for centuries. God can offer strength, give people the determination not to let this crime, this sin, beat them. Lovendale will go on..."*

Clive was impressive, it had to be said. As his interview came to an end, I looked at my watch. Time I wasn't here. I reached for the remote control as DS Penrose was shown saying the police were continuing their investigation and appealing to the public for information.

I set off to walk to the cricket pavilion, looking up at the darkening sky and zipping up my anorak. The way things were going it would be just my luck to get caught in the rain. Would sorting out the gear for Alderton's next match take my mind off what was bothering me? No chance. My thoughts returned to Emily. Would she want me to contact her mother again? How would Nadia react if I did?

I turned right onto a tarmacked path that led to the Alderton Hall Hotel half a mile ahead. I saw Paddy McCann and Dale Wilson pulling carts full of clubs along the path that ran alongside the pavilion. My journalist friend was obviously after an exclusive. Good luck with that, Dale.

A moment later my humour wasn't improved by the sight of a young woman in a floral patterned summer dress walking towards me with a yappy mongrel in tow. Olivia Brent. The one person I would normally have done anything to avoid. 'I made it clear from the start I was bi-sexual,' Nadia had said on the day she walked out on me, as if I only had a right to complain if she'd gone off with a bloke. I ignored Olivia and moved on. Nadia and her new partner lived on a new estate that was reached along a footpath that ran through the woods near the cricket ground. It had been one of my favourite walks.

An urgent need to escape had been a strong presence on and off since Nadia had left. Now it hit me like a blow. Maybe I should do the Lovendale Way again, the other way around this time. No chance of that: work tomorrow. I reached the cricket ground and skirted the boundary. Even the sight of the covers decorated with the Alderton Hall logo and five gold stars failed to raise my spirits. Then my phone rang and a woman from Castlebridge spent a good ten minutes explaining in minute detail everything she wanted in her new kitchen.

Finally arriving at the pavilion, I took out my keys, but somebody had forgotten to lock the door. I went in and, turning to the right, caught the usual smell of sweat, warm air and something else I couldn't quite identify. Paint. Of course, Tiffany was painting the walls this week. She hadn't made much progress: just the window frames had been done so far. Walking over to the three cricket bags that had been shoved in the far corner, I noticed some ladders leaning against the wall next to several tins of white gloss. I passed a couple of bats lying on benches; a discarded beer bottle resting against a pair of pads on the floor and a solitary sock sitting forlornly on top of a locker.

Having thought of Tiffany, I couldn't stop a lurid image of her and Brian having it away in the pavilion from flashing through my mind. Not a pretty sight was how Rebecca had described it. Gruesome, I would have said.

I opened up the first bag to check everything was there. Halfway through the second one, I thought I heard movement behind me. I looked round but saw nothing out of the ordinary. Must get a grip, I was imagining things now. I picked up a helmet with a hole in it, still feeling there was somebody with me. The atmosphere in the room was getting to me. Next, the sound of someone breathing seemed to come from over my right shoulder. Stop it, you've got a job to do. Finally satisfied everything was OK, I turned to leave.

In the opposite corner, half a dozen cushions had been thrown on top of a tarpaulin, which covered a kind of lump. Something was not right. I stood still for a moment, reluctant to move, then walked cautiously, like a character in a slow motion scene from a movie. I moved closer and saw two red boots sticking out from under the tarpaulin. Someone was wearing them.

"What the...?"

My voice echoed from the wooden walls. I stared stupidly for a while before realising I ought to do something. I flung the cushions away two at a time then dragged the tarpaulin off to reveal the woman underneath. I took a step back when I saw the livid marks on the neck.

Rushing outside in desperate need of air, I leant against the door jamb, afraid my legs wouldn't keep me upright for much longer. I fumbled for the mobile in my pocket, but almost dropped it. As I dialled 999, I took a couple of paces forward and managed to bang my shin against a bench. Though grimacing with pain, I must have made sense because the operator said they would send an ambulance and the police.

* * *

Some time later, I was sat on a wooden bench on a footpath about twenty yards away from the cricket square. A paramedic had looked at my shin and said, 'you'll be fine, mate'. Now Sergeant Penrose sat next to me, notebook in hand. He had told me Tiffany Booth was dead. Just as I thought. Her little boy, Harry, was only two, poor kid. Tiff's mam and dad, who doted on the little boy, would look after him. Nobody seemed to know who Harry's father was. The detective began his questioning.

"Could you take me through what happened?"

I was so befuddled I had to ask Penrose to repeat the question before I told him about seeing the boots and moving the cushions.

"Right. On the way here, did you see anybody?"

'I don't know' would have sounded stupid, but it was true. Right then, I wasn't sure of anything. Again, I thought hard and gradually remembered what had happened before I found Tiffany. I told Penrose about spotting Olivia walking her dog.

"This Olivia Brent, who is she exactly?"

"She's the woman my wife left me for."

"That must have been difficult for you," he said.

"You could say that."

He nodded.

"Did you talk to her when you saw her today?"

"What do you think?"

"I'll take that as a no. Did you see anybody else?"

"Paddy McCann and Dale Wilson, the reporter from the chronicle were off for a game of golf," I said.

There was no need to ask who McCann was. Everybody knew him. Sergeant Penrose checked what time everything had happened, then changed tack.

"Try and think back to finding the body. Was there anything you noticed?"

I closed my eyes and pictured the scene then sat back, suddenly overcome with exhaustion.

"Sorry, that's it," I said.

"Not to worry. Getting back to Tiffany. How well did you know her?"

"Well, I employed her for painting jobs now and again," I replied.

"Right. An unusual occupation for a woman, isn't it?"

"Suppose so. She only took it up last year, said she'd always wanted to do it. One day she was working in Clinton's supermarket in Loventon. Next thing you knew she was driving a brand new van and painting people's houses."

He wrote busily but I wondered how much use what I'd told him was.

"I see. Is it true you witnessed an incident involving Tiffany in the village shop a few weeks ago?"

"You heard about that, did you?"

I explained what I could remember about Rebecca's announcement to the assembled customers, Tiffany's angry response and Kate ending up on the floor.

"And your girlfriend had to go to hospital?"

"What you on about?"

"Your girlfriend, Kate George."

"I hardly know the woman."

He gave me a knowing look.

"Oh, right. I thought with you taking her to hospital and having coffee with her..."

"I was just being a good neighbour."

"Sure. Now then, you definitely heard Rebecca Lumley accuse Tiffany Booth of having an affair with her husband?"

"Yeah, so did several other people."

Penrose's face gave nothing away as he wrote in his notebook, tapping it with his pen when he'd finished.

"When did you last see Tiffany?"

"I don't know really, probably not for a week or so, but I talked to her on the phone a few days ago about a job in Bentley."

"Is there anything else you can tell me?"

"No, sorry. My head's all over the place."

"Yeah. It's a shock, I know. Thanks for your help. I'll need to see how they're getting on inside the pavilion."

With an instruction to give him a call if I thought of anything else, he went on his way.

* * *

At eight o'clock I began to walk home. I hadn't gone far when my phone rang.

"Hi, it's Richard Keppler here," said the caller.

"Richard...?"

The name rang a vague bell.

"I've booked the flat. I think it was your daughter I spoke to when I made the reservation."

"Right. How can I help you?"

"I'm in the village now, outside the tea shop."

Oh, hell, finding Tiffany had made me forget he was arriving today.

"I'll be with you in five minutes."

When I got to *Tea Time* a man with dark, curly hair was waiting on the pavement.

"Richard Keppler?"

"Yeah, you must be...?"

"Sam Flint, welcome to Lovendale."

He smiled and shook my hand. As we walked the few yards to the flat, Richard commented on how peaceful Alderton seemed.

"It's just what I need. I've got a novel to finish."

"Yeah? What sort of things do you write?"

I glanced at him out of the corner of my eye.

"Crime, mostly."

I made a mental note to look for his books.

"The thing is, Sam, I don't want to be disturbed. So if anybody comes looking for me, you haven't seen me, OK?"

A headache throbbed away around my temples on the way home. The effect of the Lovendale Way had worn off by now and I felt more stressed out than ever. Within a few days we'd had two murders. Was the same person responsible for both deaths? If so, that led inevitably to one dreadful question: who would be next?

PART TWO

LOVERS IN A DANGEROUS TIME

CHAPTER SIXTEEN

"Hello, Jacob," said Penny, taking her son from Emily's lap, "have you had a nice time?"

Her face lit up as usual at the sight of him. Considering he was adopted, Jacob bore a remarkable resemblance to Penny, having her red hair and blue eyes. She smiled in Emily's direction.

"Thank you for stepping into the breech," said Penny. "I can't think what became of Tiffany."

"No bother. We've had a great time, haven't we, Jacob?"

Jacob babbled in reply. Penny listened with great interest to her boy's prattle about Peppa Pig as the DVD played on.

"Is that the time?" said Penny, looking at her watch. "The meeting ran on. Why can't people shut up occasionally? That's the last time I ask Tiffany Booth for help. Letting me down like that. A thirty second phone call, that's all it would have taken."

"I know."

"And I have no idea where Clive is. Some church business I expect, unless he's playing golf again. He's hardly ever in these days."

"Must be busy, I guess."

"Hmm. I'm busy too, nobody seems to think about that."

"This is it, like."

"Listen to me going on about Clive, I must be putting you off marriage. Anyway, how's your dad these days, Emily?"

"Fine."

"I thought he would have had a girlfriend by now."

"He might do for all I know. We don't talk about that sort of thing."

Penny nodded.

"He's such a good neighbour," she said. "He was the first person I thought of when I needed someone to talk to after finding Dawn."

"It must have been hard."

"Yes."

They sat in silence for a while. Emily sneaked a glance at her watch.

"I need to be off, Penny," she said. "I'm working at the Bricklayers soon."

"You're not going out with Mark tonight?"

She shook her head.

"No, he's having a drink with friends."

* * *

As Emily rushed off, she wondered why married women were always slagging off their husbands. After a moment's thought she decided it was worth listening to Penny moaning for the sake of the tenner she pressed into her hand for watching telly with her dead cute little boy for an hour. It was a nice bonus to add to what the landlord of the Bricklayers would be paying her tonight. All cash in hand as well.

Her mind went back to what Penny had said about Sam. She was only yards away from the pub when it hit her: Penny Wheatley fancied her dad. Emily had got used to Penny popping round on some pretext or other. That couldn't be just because Dad was 'a good neighbour'? She almost giggled at the thought of it, imagining their names chalked in a heart on the schoolyard wall: Penny Loves Sam. Then again, why not? Not that Penny would stand much of a chance.

Emily just made it in time for her shift behind the bar. She needed to be busy tonight after her mum had let her down again. She should be used to it by now. Deep down she knew it was something she would never fully accept. Having looked into it in some depth, she had learned the most common form of abuse wasn't sexual; it was neglect, usually fuelled by some form of addiction.

The question, 'why me?' nagged away at her. If she had a pound for all the times someone had told her it wasn't her fault, she wouldn't have to be a part-time barmaid. Knowing she wasn't responsible for her mum's bad behaviour didn't stop guilt from eating her up. Whoever's fault it was, on bad days she felt like damaged goods. That was one of the things that drove her to do well at school, to achieve something with her life, to prove she was basically OK. University would be a part of that.

A regular stream of customers stopped her brooding too much. Blokes delaying their return to their wives came up to order 'one last pint'; couples who had booked tables puzzled over the menu as if making some sort of life-changing decision; a group of ten commandeered a long table at the back of the bar. They would send the noise levels through the roof later.

Emily had often thought the Bricklayers was a weird mixture. A cardboard cut-out of Dusty Springfield by the door welcomed punters as they arrived; hunting prints adorned the walls; customers who weren't eating sat in battered but comfortable armchairs in alcoves. Now, as she looked over to the door, Mark walked in, a big grin on his face.

"Hello, Emily," he said, rubbing his hands.

"Hi, what are you doing here?"

"I've come to see you of course."

"That's nice. I thought you were out with the lads tonight."

He shook his head.

"I could have done but I didn't fancy it. Why not walk into Alderton and see the love of my life, I thought? And have a pint of course. Carlsberg, please."

While Emily was getting Mark's lager, Clive Wheatley came in with Paddy McCann. The vicar ordered two pints of Bentley Special Bitter, using its full title. Everyone else called it BSB.

"Did you see Clive on the telly tonight, Emily?" asked Paddy as she pulled the first pint.

Mark got in quick in that laddish way of his.

"What was it, Paddy, *I'm a Celebrity Get Me Out of Here?*"

She tried not to laugh too loud; Paddy chuckled; Clive looked uncomfortable.

"No, but I wouldn't rule it out, Mark. The rev here could become famous after his performance on the local news."

"Oh, yes?"

"Interviewed by the lovely Lita Bridge no less."

"Some guys have all the luck," said Mark.

"You'll be making your girlfriend jealous, saying things like that."

Emily passed over the first beer, which Clive took gratefully. He drank while his companions continued their banter.

"She knows I'm only joking, don't you, Emily?"

"So if Lita Bridge walked in now and offered you her body, you'd turn her down, would you?" she said.

"How do women do it, lads?" asked Mark, a look of wide-eyed innocence on his face. "How do they think of the most difficult question to ask a guy?"

Paddy came to his rescue.

"Anyway, back to our local TV star. Our Clive talked about this murder and how badly it's affected everyone. Very eloquent he was."

Clive responded to Paddy's praise with suitable modesty.

"Oh, I don't know about that. Just did my job. It was an extension of what I did at the funeral. A little more public, that's all."

"I bet you enjoyed every minute of it," said Paddy.

"Not a bit of it. I hate media work. It's Penny who pushes it. She's always beavering away in the background. Now she's put her high-flying career on hold, she wants me to be all dynamic. Not really me, I'm afraid."

"No?"

"I'm quite happy with things as they are. Penny's quite the opposite, always looking for the next challenge, the next project."

Emily handed over Paddy's pint and took the cash from Clive. The men stood at the bar for a bit longer, indulging in idle chat.

"I think I'll nip in the garden for a smoke," said Paddy.

"I'll join you, mate," said Mark, "need a bit of air, been indoors all day."

He followed Paddy out, giving his girlfriend a wink on the way.

"Yes, good idea, Mark," said Clive, following suit.

Moments after they had left, a familiar looking woman came in and approached the bar.

"Hello, Emily," she said, "I didn't know you worked here."

It was the CID woman who had interviewed her in the shop. Her hair was loose this time, it suited her better.

"Just now and again."

"Any chance of a coffee? With cream?"

"Sure."

While Emily got the coffee, DC Travis sat on a bar stool.

"I've been to Loventon on a case, I'm just on the way home. I decided I'd expire without a caffeine injection."

Emily put the cup and a jug of cream on the bar.

"I thought you would have been out with your boyfriend on a Friday night."

"Well, he is here but decided to go into the garden for some reason. He said he'd come to see me, but then decided he needed fresh air, though he walked here and will only be breathing in cigarette smoke."

DC Travis shrugged.

"No point in trying to understand men, Emily. Your boyfriend, he's not the good-looking one I met in the shop that day, is he? Mark."

"Yes."

"Nice one."

The constable poured cream in the coffee and took a sip.

"Mmm, that's good. I don't suppose you've remembered anything else about Dawn Fraser that might help me, have you?"

"Sorry. No arrest yet then?"

"Not yet, but getting there, you know. The time when you saw her was crucial. Did she say anything about where she was planning to go that night or the next day?"

"She was going to have an early night, I do know that. She wanted to leave about half seven the next morning. She would be heading south."

Emily thought about the conversation she'd had with Dawn Fraser on the day she died. She'd been so looking forward to going away, really up for it. It was no good asking about where she planned to go. Whether she was heading south or north hardly mattered. One thing was for sure. She never got there.

CHAPTER SEVENTEEN

Mark, Paddy and Clive managed to find a table in the pub garden. Mark was glad of a chance to talk to Paddy. There was no harm in trying to impress an Avanatta board member. Pity Clive had to tag along.

"See, the thing is, Paddy," said Mark, "everybody goes on about shopping online, the death of the high street and that, but people still like to go into a real live shop and talk to a human being."

"I do so agree," said Clive. "Human contact is so lacking in today's world, you have young people wasting their lives staring at screens..."

"Human contact, you've hit the nail right on the head, Clive. That's what I said to my gaffer the day I started at the Avanatta shop."

Paddy took a sip from his pint and flicked ash into the ashtray on the table.

"Whatever you're doing, it's working," he said. "Sales have gone through the roof in the past few months."

Mark grabbed his chance.

"Well, I like to think I've injected a bit of dynamism into the organisation. Not that I want to blow my own trumpet."

"If you don't do it, nobody else will," said Paddy.

Mark laughed sycophantically.

"I can see why you've been so successful, Paddy."

A woman came out of the back door of the Bricklayers and walked towards them. Mark's heart sank when he recognised her. She stopped at their table and took an ID badge from her handbag.

"Mr Hanwell? DC Travis, Lovendale CID. Sorry to bother you, but I wonder if I could have a quick word."

"Sure."

"Perhaps we could find somewhere at the back that's a bit more private."

Mark got up and walked with the detective away from his companions. They faced one another at a rickety table.

"Now, Mr Hanwell, a car similar to one registered in your name was seen in Alderton on Friday, 27th May."

"Oh, yes?"

He looked deep in thought, taking a mouthful of lager.

"Were you driving through the village on that day?"

"I could have been, not really sure to be honest."

"Were you at work that day?"

"Probably. I have a different day off every week, so it's hard to say."

The detective constable looked straight into his eyes as if trying to outstare him.

"Your manager says you left the shop where you work at three thirty that afternoon to take some stock to a shop in Castlebridge."

He smiled.

"I remember now. We'd received an order meant for Castlebridge – you'll never believe it but they got a consignment of phones meant for us a few days later. No wonder the economy's in such a mess."

"I've looked at the map and I wouldn't have thought the quickest route is via Alderton."

"Going the long way round isn't a crime, is it, detective?"

"Of course not, but…"

"I thought I'd take my time, enjoy the countryside. It was a beautiful day. I was going straight home after I'd dropped the phones off so I was in no hurry."

She joined her hands together, interlocking the fingers.

"You realise the 27th of May was the day Dawn Fraser was killed?"

His eyes opened in mock surprise.

"Was it? I can remember hearing about it but not the exact date."

"We put out a request for anyone who was in the vicinity of Alderton at the relevant time to come forward."

"Sorry, must have missed that."

"It was on the radio, telly, local paper."

He shrugged.

"Well, there you go. I avoid the news. Too depressing."

She looked sceptical.

"Did you know Mrs Fraser?"

"Not really. I'd met her in this pub just before Christmas. Emily, my girlfriend, introduced us."

"What did you think of her?"

He drank more lager.

"She seemed all right, you know. She'd had a few drinks I remember."

The detective constable tapped the table and looked as if she was trying to remember her next question.

"Do you remember anything she said?"

He shrugged.

"Not really, it's a few months ago now."

"Would you say she was attractive?"

"She wasn't bad looking, I suppose, quite a bit older than me so it's hard to judge."

"Only we've heard she had a toy-boy."

"I don't know what you're insinuating, but you're way off beam."

"I'm only…"

Mark had had enough.

"I know what this is about, detective. It's because of my family, isn't it?"

"Your f...?"

"Oh, he's one of the Hanwells, they're notorious, they are. Live on Moor Park, need I say more?"

"Mr Hanwell, I assure you..."

"Save it. How do you think it looked, eh? A copper approaching me in a public place. I bet you wouldn't have treated Councillor McCann like that. Or the Reverend Wheatley. You would have made an appointment, everything nice and discreet."

"I know nothing about your family..."

"Pull the other one, it sings *God Save the Queen*. You can't be bothered doing a proper investigation, just nab the nearest chav. Well, I'm not a chav, I'm a human being, entitled to respect like anyone else."

He got up, glass in hand.

"I'm trying to make something of my life if you lot will let me. Now I'm going back to my friends. If you need me again, give me a call at the shop and I'll see if I can spare you five minutes."

He walked away, well pleased with the way he'd handled himself. He'd made it clear how angry he was to be picked on because of his background, but hadn't lost his temper.

When the detective had been asking about Dawn, he'd stuck as close to the truth as he could, always a good tactic. At the same time, he'd have to watch himself. How much did she know about him and Dawn? Had some toerag been spreading rumours? It was a good job he hadn't sent any texts, e-mails or tweets. He always made sure nothing could be traced.

If anyone knew about him and Dawn, he could be dragged in for more questioning about her murder. Worse still, Emily might find out. That must be avoided at all costs.

CHAPTER EIGHTEEN

On her way through the village to her dad's holiday flat on Saturday morning, Emily was distracted by thoughts of what he had told her about Tiffany. Another murder in Alderton. It was all getting out of hand.

Getting to 17, The Green, she rang the bell of the apartment. Richard Keppler opened the door. He was wearing a navy-blue dressing gown.

"Good morning, Richard. Sorry to bother you. I'm Emily Flint, Sam's daughter. He asked me to call round to check you were all right."

"Oh, hiya, Emily. I can see the family resemblance. Come in."

They walked through the hallway into the kitchen and sat down.

"Is everything OK with the flat?" she asked.

"Yeah, sure, couldn't be better."

"There's nothing else you need?"

He shrugged.

"No, it's just perfect."

She nodded, satisfied she had done her duty by Flint Apartments, aka her dad, who paid her for this sort of thing.

"Well, I'll be off, leave you to it."

As they both got up, they heard footsteps outside the door. Emily turned to see a woman come in.

"Richard, are you...?"

She was wearing nothing but a red T-shirt just long enough to cover the essentials. On it was written *Careful or you might end up in my next novel.* It wasn't the garment itself or the logo that attracted Emily's attention. It was the woman who was wearing it.

"Hello, Mum," she said. "All right?"

Richard's jaw dropped. He looked from mother to daughter and back again.

"Nadia, what...?"

She ignored him, turning to address Emily.

"There's no need to tell Olivia about this."

"Olivia? I don't think I know her, let me think now."

Emily made a performance of putting her hand under her chin and pondering some tricky problem.

"Oh, you mean Miss Brent. Richard, do you know my mum, like, ran off with my English teacher?"

The novelist looked on, helpless. He said nothing. Emily moved in for the kill.

"Has she had a drink today?"

Richard looked bemused.

"A bit early, isn't it?"

"Me and my big mouth," said Emily, clapping her hand over her mouth. "I thought she would have told you about her drink problem. You know, 'My name is Nadia and I'm an alcoholic'."

Nadia looked daggers at her.

"I thought I'd brought you up to be a bit more discreet."

Emily snorted with contempt.

"You never brought me up. That was down to Dad and Grandma and Granddad. Heaven knows where I'd be without them."

"I don't think Richard wants to hear all this..."

"Oh, I think he does. We're giving him ideas for his next book. This whole conversation could be out of a drama. Richard's the new guy trying to catch up with the backstory."

Richard decided to cut her short.

"I really think we should…"

He had achieved the impossible and looked even more uncomfortable.

"I bet you thought this was a sleepy little valley in the middle of nowhere, didn't you?" said Emily. "No way."

"Emily, please…"

She took no notice of her mother's attempt to silence her.

"There's all sorts that goes on round here but let's concentrate on the matter in hand: a nice little domestic dispute. A writer's dream."

As Emily stopped speaking, the three of them looked at one another as if waiting for someone to say something. After a minute or so, Emily began to walk away before turning to Richard.

"What do you think then? Is there enough material there? Mum and I would be, like, the main characters. Think it would work?"

That would have to do as an exit line, she said to herself on the way back home. The satisfaction at having got the better of her mother in an argument wouldn't last. Already tears were streaming down her face, questions without answers battering her brain. Why did Mum do these things? Showing her own daughter up like that – showing herself up. She might say nobody would find out, but she was hoping somebody would find out – anything to get a reaction.

* * *

By five o'clock, Emily didn't know what to do with herself. She'd been looking forward to a weekend off; now she wished she was at work. When she had first got back home, she had tried displacement activity. Having already put a load of washing in the machine, ironed three pairs of jeans and tidied her room, she turned to reading.

Now she lay on her bed, making a futile attempt to read *Harry Potter and the Order of the Phoenix*. She'd decided to re-read the whole series and had raced through the first four books, getting halfway through number five at the same breath-taking pace, but today she couldn't settle into anything. Nothing would shift the picture of her mum in that obscene T-shirt from her mind. She needed to confront her, tell her exactly what she thought of her, cut her out of her life once and for all. It would be easier once she was in London, but she had to start now.

Jumping off the bed, Emily put on her trainers and got her coat. Moments later, she was out in the fresh air, feeling the breeze on her face. Now she had a plan, things didn't seem so bad. Walking briskly past the *Bricklayers* she turned left past the shop, glancing in the window. Richard Keppler was just reaching up for a packet of biscuits. Luckily, he had his back to Emily. Going on towards the village green, she approached the holiday flat. Keppler being out only made her task easier. She had to see Mum on her own.

Ringing the bell for the ground floor apartment, she paced up and down. No answer. She tried again, keeping her finger on the bell. Nobody in. Emily had no intention of going to her mum's new home. No way was she going to risk meeting the lovely Olivia. Sighing, she was about to leave when she heard somebody moving about at the back and a gate opening. After a moment's thought, she walked round the side of the house to take a look.

There was nobody in the back garden, but somebody in a red hoody was sprinting down the path towards the Lovendale Hills. It looked like they had gone through the gate in the back fence, which had been left open.

Emily went over to the window of the flat and looked in. Seeing Mum slumped on the armchair, she knew straight away what had happened. Rather than talk things over with Keppler, she'd had a skinful then passed out. He must have decided to leave her to it. Who could blame him?

She had a key and could have gone in to wake her, but discarded the idea. There would be no chance of getting any sense out of her. Watching the pathetic figure in the chair, dead to the world, she almost felt sorry for her. What a life she must have. She had a job, but how much longer would she be able to hang onto it? Separated from her loving husband, estranged from her only child, she filled her time by getting drunk and shagging around. Olivia Brent wouldn't put up with her much longer. Shaking her head sorrowfully, Emily saw the idea of confrontation for what it was: petty and demeaning for both of them.

As she rushed away, Emily banged her handbag against the picnic table, knocking it onto the bench, where some of the contents spilled out. Cursing silently, she stooped to pick up her purse, phone and a packet of Tampax. She stuffed them back in the bag, which had landed on some sort of wire and wood contraption. It had somehow wrapped itself round the bag. With more cursing she took hold of it in both hands and threw it angrily onto the grass. Then she walked away.

CHAPTER NINETEEN

In the nets behind Alderton Hall Hotel, Kate played a sweetly timed on drive. For a moment she admired her shot, then surveyed the scene around her. Across the golf course, over the trees and beyond the bend in the river, the ever present Lovendale Hills dominated the landscape. It had to be one of the best settings for cricket practice or for anything else.

She had stayed the previous night with a friend in Lincoln and had got back late for the Saturday practice, stressed out by the long drive. Immediately on arriving, she had relaxed. Over the past four weeks, she had got used to the slow pace of life in Alderton. The weather had helped. It looked set to be a glorious summer. Then DS Penrose walked up to spoil it.

"Damn and blast it," she said half out loud as the officer got nearer.

"Hello, Kate," he said. "Any chance of a word?"

She removed her helmet and faced the policeman. He was wearing his inevitable brown suit; somehow, in her maroon and black Alderton Cricket Club T-shirt, shorts and trainers, she felt at a disadvantage.

"Can't it wait, Sergeant? I'm busy at the moment."

"I'm afraid it's urgent."

After making her excuses to her teammates, she removed her pads and went off with Penrose.

"I didn't know you were a cricketer," he said.

"I've played for years. I could never imagine life without cricket."

"I presume you're a member of Alderton CC."

"Yes. Sam, my neighbour, took me along a couple of weeks ago. I paid my subs, had a few practices and got picked for the women's team. The usual opening bat was on maternity leave."

They sat at a picnic table on the edge of the golf course. The DS took out a notebook from his jacket pocket. Polite conversation was at an end. Now it was official.

"Do you know Tiffany Booth?" he asked.

"I don't think so."

"I was under the impression you did know her. Weren't you involved in an incident with Ms Booth in the village shop?"

"That Tiffany? What a strange thing to ask about. I wouldn't say I know her."

"Nevertheless, there was an altercation, was there not?"

"I'd hardly describe it as an altercation. I think I could be called an innocent bystander."

"What exactly happened?"

Wasn't the murder of Dawn Fraser more important than a stupid little incident like this?

"Does it matter? It was weeks ago, an accident, no harm done. I'd just as soon forget about it."

He looked at her for a moment, his expression unreadable.

"If you could go through it for me."

"Perhaps you wouldn't mind telling me what this is all about."

The sergeant took his time coming to a decision.

"You mean you don't know?"

"No."

"I thought your teammates would have told you."

"I was late, I've hardly had time to talk to anybody."

Again, there was a pause. Kate tapped her foot in irritation.

"Didn't you see the crime scene as you passed the cricket pitch?"

"Crime scene," she repeated, shaking her head, "no, I drove in the back way."

"Tiffany Booth's body was found in Alderton cricket pavilion last night."

"She's dead?"

"I'm afraid so."

"Oh, God. Poor girl."

"Any information you can give us could be important."

"Of course."

Kate explained about the argument between Tiffany and Rebecca and what followed.

"Have you seen either Tiffany or Rebecca since then?" asked the DS.

"I've seen them about the village but haven't spoken to them."

"What's your feeling about the incident now?"

Kate thought back to the moment she collided with the freezer, felt again the pain in her head and the excruciating embarrassment when she was sick.

"Nothing much. At the time one felt rather foolish, I suppose."

"You weren't angry?"

"I didn't have time for that. I was spark out for a time. When I came round, I hadn't enough energy left to be angry."

"I see. Where were you last night?"

"In Lincoln."

"Lincoln?"

"Yes, you know, it's a city in Lincolnshire…"

"I know where it is, thank you. What were you doing there?"

"I spent the night with a friend. The traffic on the A1 was horrendous this morning, which was why I got back late."

"We'll need the contact details for your friend."

"You mean…? Oh, sure."

She gave him the information he'd asked for.

"This is the first time I've been considered as a suspect, but I guess at this stage of the investigation nothing can be ruled out."

"Quite."

When Sergeant Penrose had noted down the details, he took a card from his inside pocket and handed it to Kate.

"If you think of anything else, please call me on that number. Any time."

Another murder. The same person must have killed Tiffany and Dawn. But who? And why?

* * *

That evening, Kate was determined to relax. She didn't want to talk to anybody or do anything but sit and read, maybe watch telly over a glass of wine. The visit from the police had disturbed her equilibrium. She needed some time on her own to process the new information but wouldn't you know it, the doorbell rang about quarter to eight. Kate shook her head in disbelief. Couldn't people just leave her alone?

"Come in," she said to Rebecca Lumley.

Her invitation lacked enthusiasm. Kate offered her visitor a seat in the living room and sat on an armchair opposite her.

"I'm sorry to barge in on you like this, Kate, but I wondered if you had heard about Tiffany."

"Yes, terrible, isn't it?"

"Of course. The thing is, Kate, I've had the police round."

"So have I."

"I wondered if they'd want to see you. I suppose they wanted to know about what happened in the shop that day."

A smile of complicity passed across her face.

"The police have to take it seriously, but we can laugh about it now."

"I'm afraid I have no desire to laugh about spending my first night in Lovendale in hospital."

"Oh? Oh, right. Anyway, I was about to say, I had to provide an alibi for the time of Tiffany's death," she said. "Luckily, I was in the office at the relevant time."

After the merest pause for breath, Rebecca whinged on.

"I can't believe they suspect me."

"Really?"

"Anyway, Kate, I'd never do time for that silly bitch. I wasn't happy about her and Brian. It was embarrassing for a start. Couldn't he at least have picked someone with a bit more class?"

"Well, I…"

"As for choosing the pavilion for a lover's tryst, how tacky can you get? Too bloody mean to take the girl to a hotel."

"I really am rather busy…"

"When I think of all I've done for him. I work all the hours God sends to subsidise that business. Well, no more. I've left the two-timing rat, got myself a nice flat in Loventon. Filed for divorce. By the time I've finished with him, he'll be sorry he was ever born."

"Will the police be back to see you?"

"Your guess is as good as mine, Kate. They'll be checking out my alibi."

"Naturally."

"They wanted to know if anybody could confirm that I was at work that day. I had to give them the names of my secretary, colleagues, even the cleaner for heaven's sake."

"At least Penrose is making a thorough job of it."

"I was in my own office alone for a couple of hours in the afternoon. Catching up on paperwork, letters, VAT returns, an accountant's work is never done."

She was running out of steam.

"DC Travis was trying to insinuate I could have nipped out, killed Tiffany and got back with nobody any the wiser."

CHAPTER TWENTY

About twenty-four hours after I had found Tiffany, I knocked on the door of number thirteen, a parcel addressed to Kate in my hand. A good thing I'd been working all day and had something to take my mind off the body. Kate, as elegant as ever in a black and white dress, came to the door.

"Hello, Sam," she said with a smile.

I held out the parcel.

"Hiya. This came yesterday. The postman asked me to take it in for you. Sorry, I forgot all about it until now."

"Oh, that's all right. Come in."

I followed her into the lounge.

"Just put the parcel on the table for now. Thanks. Sit down unless you're dashing off somewhere."

"No, I'm not going anywhere."

I sat on the settee. She sat beside me.

"I haven't seen you for a couple of days," she said.

"We live so near one another yet we only seem to meet at the cricket club. Have you been doing much?"

"I'm quite pleased with myself at the moment. I got a part-time job the other day."

"Well done. What's the job?"

"It's with *Lovendale Cottages*, a day and a half a week, taking bookings, answering the phone, all that stuff. I saw an advert in the village shop so I went round to make inquiries."

That meant she was going to stay for a while, good news as far as I was concerned.

"Great. I'm afraid my news isn't so good. Have you heard about Tiffany?"

"Yes. The police came to see me in the middle of cricket practice. Have they been to see you?"

"You could say that. I found the body."

"Oh, Sam. I thought you were looking a bit fed up. It must have been awful."

I shrugged.

"Not nice, no, but at least I'm still here, unlike poor Tiffany."

"What happened?"

I thought I might find it hard to talk about it. Instead, once I started, I was glad of the opportunity to go through the events of the previous night. I told her about walking to the cricket ground, going into the pavilion and finding Tiffany.

"Ghastly," said Kate. "Are you OK?"

"Yeah, fine. You know, Kate, I feel involved in what's happened somehow. What the hell's going on?"

"Good question."

"Tiffany had all these marks, bruises, whatever round her throat. They reminded me of what Penny said about Dawn."

"Well, looking at it logically, the same person must have killed both women. Who could be doing this? There's a lot going on beneath the surface of people's lives. One knew that already, but I suppose recent events confirm it."

"You're right there, Kate, though in Alderton lately it's been well above the surface. That fight between Tiff and Rebecca in the shop is a case in point. The police seemed very interested in it when they spoke to me. They must consider Rebecca a suspect."

"I should think so. Rebecca came to see me earlier, obviously wanting to find out what I'd told DS Penrose."

I couldn't believe Rebecca Lumley or anyone I knew would actually kill anyone, but someone had killed Tiffany. Kate went through what the police had asked her.

"This could get depressing," she said after a bit more speculation about the murders. "Let's cheer ourselves up. Do you fancy a glass of wine?"

"Good idea. Thanks."

While she was out, I looked round the room, taking in the leather settee, an ethnic looking rug and a mirror above the fireplace. Art deco maybe. Or was it art nouveau? I picked up a CD from the coffee table and began to read the song list on the back.

"This is a golden oldie," I said, as Kate returned and put a bottle and two glasses on the table.

"Yes, I love Bare Naked Ladies."

"Funnily enough, so do I."

Was that a hint of a blush on her face?

"Oh, my God," she said, "did I really say that?"

"I'm afraid you did. Anyway, I haven't listened to them for ages. Can we play it?"

"Sure."

I watched Kate walk over to the CD player in that smooth, sensuous way of hers. She joined in with the first track, *Old Apartment,* as she sat down again.

"This one came out when I was doing A levels. I used to play it while I was revising."

"You must be older than you look."

"One certainly hopes so."

She picked up the wine bottle.

"Now, I reckon you're a Malbec man."

"How do you know?"

She shrugged, twisting the screw top.

"Just a knack. I can look at anyone and say straight away what their favourite wine is."

I grinned at her.

"Amazing."

She poured the wine.

"A nice drop," I said.

"Are you a bit of a wine buff then?"

I took a sip and rolled the wine round my tongue.

"Oh, yeah. I know all about aroma, tannins, statins...."

"Statins? Aren't they what you take for high cholesterol?"

"How should I know? With wine there's only one question you need to ask: is it on special offer?"

"I'll drink to that."

We clinked glasses.

"Before I heard about Tiffany," said Kate, "I thought things might be settling down. No such luck."

"I reckon things started to go pear-shaped when Rebecca made that announcement in the shop."

"We'll blame her then, shall we? What do you think of her?"

I thought for a moment, without coming to any definite conclusion.

"I don't know her very well, although she's Nadia's boss."

"Nadia? Is that your wife?"

I nodded.

"What does she think of Rebecca?"

I thought of Nadia's constant moans about her boss.

"Reckons she will do anything to get a reaction. Attention-seeking, you know."

Though that was a case of the pot calling the kettle black if ever there was one.

"Rebecca's not a friend of yours?"

I shook my head, Kate drank more wine before going on.

"When she came to talk about Tiffany, I got the impression she had something to hide."

"Maybe she has."

"One could say we all have, though she was quite frank about certain things."

"Such as?"

"Her husband. She says she's going to divorce him."

"No surprise there."

I'd always thought Brian was a nondescript sort of bloke – Emily said he was creepy – yet he'd attracted both Rebecca and Tiffany. Kate twirled a lock of hair round her finger.

"I've not had time to get really friendly with anybody around here but I already know so much about some people I've met. The kind of private stuff they'd never have told me under normal circumstances."

Normal circumstances, what were they? Would they ever come back? While I struggled with unanswerable questions, Kate elaborated.

"I'm like an observer, a voyeur almost. I've sort of soaked up lots of information without making the slightest effort."

"Didn't you come up here for a bit of peace?"

"No chance of that. Anyway, I'm not sure the quiet life would suit me. I'm used to being busy, being around people, having things to think about."

"You've got plenty to think about now."

She smiled.

"And how. It's all whirling round in my head a bit. I must confess it's interesting to see a police investigation from the other side."

"Suppose it must be."

"Anyway, I was thinking of having something to eat. You're welcome to join me if you don't mind pizza from the village shop."

"That'll do me," I said. "Thanks."

We had pizza and salad, more wine and more chat. After we'd listened to the last BNL track, *Lovers in a Dangerous Time,* and finished the bottle, Kate suggested a walk by the river. Outside, having drunk more than I was used to, I was feeling pleasantly mellow. It was nice to be out walking with an attractive woman.

"Have you been back to London since you arrived in Alderton?" I asked.

"No, I don't seem to have had time. I'm going to see my parents tomorrow."

"You must miss your family and friends."

She nodded.

"I guess so, not as much as I thought. Lovendale is better for after dinner strolls."

"Do you do much walking?"

"Not the really serious stuff. Something like this is fine by me. If I want exercise, I go to the gym."

"I did the Lovendale Way a few weeks ago."

"I remember you telling the police that. What is it exactly?"

I explained.

"Sounds like hard work."

"Yeah but it's brilliant. Makes you feel good, keeps you fit, clears your head. You can't beat it. And it's the only way to appreciate the countryside."

She gave me a sceptical look.

"Mmm, not so sure about that."

"Just you wait, you won't be here long before you get kitted out, boots, kagoule, woolly hat, the lot."

"Yeah, right."

We walked on a bit, turning back after a mile where the Loven met its tributary, the Kenser.

"I keep meaning to have a look at the church," said Kate. "It looks interesting."

"We can go now if you like."

We approached St Gregory's along a paved path. Five fat yew bushes on either side stood like obese guards of honour. The subtle pinky browns of the church's sandstone, each stone randomly combined in an asymmetrical pattern, glinted in the sun.

"We need to go through this kissing gate," I said.

Kate went through first and turned to me.

"Kissing gate, is that what it's called?"

We stopped for a while and looked at one another. Her lips may have parted slightly, so might mine.

"Yeah."

After a couple of seconds our heads moved closer together and we were kissing. When we came up for air, we had our arms wrapped round one another.

"This is a surprise," I said.

"A nice one, I hope."

"Getting nicer by the second."

I kissed her again, then she whispered in my ear.

"This might be the time to invite you back for coffee."

Admiring the church was put off for a while, it seemed.

* * *

Once we got back in the house, we kissed again in the hallway. She took my hand and led me upstairs – coffee was postponed too. Then we were in bed and Kate was doing interesting things with her tongue.

"Do you still like bare naked ladies?" she murmured.

"I certainly like this one."

"The bare naked man's not so bad either."

Was my luck changing at last? Before I had a chance to consider this question, I heard a sound downstairs, a gentle tapping. I ignored it. It got louder. Soon it became an insistent banging on the front door. Kate looked at me and sighed.

"Hell, what now? One can't even have a shag in peace. I'll just get rid of them."

She jumped out of bed and threw her clothes back on. Leaning towards me, she gave me a little pat.

"Keep it warm for me."

When Kate came back in, she looked anxious.

"It's the police. Sergeant Penrose with a DC, he wants to talk to you."

How did they know I was there? A second's thought told me it was a silly question. Anybody could have seen us snogging on the river path.

"Talk to me? What about?"

And why now? A few moments of pleasure, was that all I was to be allowed? I might have known it was too good to last.

"He wouldn't tell me."

I got out of bed, knowing it was bad news. Pulling on my jeans and shirt, I followed Kate downstairs.

In the living room, a woman with fair hair in a pony-tail sat with a notebook in her hand. Sergeant Penrose looked stern by her side.

"Mr Flint," he said.

Kate and I exchanged a glance, then sat together on the settee. She took my hand. The DS spoke.

"This is DC Lindsey Travis. We're, er... I'm afraid this isn't going to be easy."

That was when I knew it was serious.

"It's about your wife, Nadia Harding. I'm sorry to tell you she's dead."

Nothing registered at first.

"What are you talking about?"

"I'm sorry, I'm afraid it's true."

The word 'true' was what convinced me. I thought of Emily first, the day she was born. Then of meeting Nadia for the first time when I was working on her parents' kitchen. A painful constriction in my stomach and chest gave way to an overwhelming sadness. I brushed a tear from my face.

"She's dead? But... what...?"

"She died earlier today. Her body was found in a flat at number seventeen The Green, Alderton."

"Does Emily know?"

"Emily?"

"Sam's daughter," put in Kate. "I take it she hasn't been told."

"Not yet."

"I need to see her," I said.

"Where is she?"

"At home, she..."

Penrose wouldn't let me finish.

"We'll get somebody to tell her soon, don't worry..."

"But she needs to hear it from me."

I made to get up.

"It's OK, Sam," said Kate, placing a comforting hand on my arm.

I sat down again.

"But..."

"It's better this way," Kate insisted. "Whoever goes to see Emily will handle it in the right way."

She turned to Penrose.

"How did she die?"

"Details are unclear at the minute, but we're treating her death as suspicious."

I knew what that meant. Murder. Three people dead now. Then I replayed something Penrose had said, realising the significance of where Nadia was found.

"17 The Green, did you say? That's my place. It's converted into flats. There's somebody staying there now. Richard something..."

I felt my lips tremble as I spoke. It took quite an effort to stop my hands from shaking.

"We are aware of that. It was Mr Keppler who found your wife."

I shook my head and flopped back on the settee.

"I don't understand. What the... she had no reason to be in the flat."

Kate stroked my hand.

"I need to ask you a few questions," said Penrose.

"OK."

"Can you tell me your movements since early this morning, Sam?"

I came out of shock for long enough to make a stab at answering the question.

"I was working on a kitchen in Bentley from about eight o'clock this morning until about half four, I suppose."

"Do you normally work Saturdays?"

"When I have to."

The sergeant asked for the name and address of the customer and who I was working with.

"Did you leave the customer's house at any time?"

"Yeah. I sat on the village green to eat my sandwiches about, what, half twelve, quarter to one. I got some stuff from B&Q in Loventon, got there about half one, would have been back just after two."

"And when you got home from work?"

"Stayed in until about seven, then came round to Kate's."

"We've been together since then," said Kate. "And if you want to know where I've been all day, I got up about eight, went into Loventon shopping. Came back around ten thirty. Went to the village shop briefly. I went to the gym at Alderton Hall Hotel about three o'clock. Came home around four fifteen. Then Rebecca Lumley dropped in at sixish, stayed perhaps half an hour. Later Sam came round."

"I'm afraid I shall have to ask you to identify your wife's body, Sam."

That was the second time he had got on first name terms. Was that significant? I got up and looked down at my bare feet.

"I'll just, er..."

I went upstairs and came back fully dressed.

"Right."

"Do you want me to come with you?" asked Kate.

I was touched by her concern but didn't know how to respond. Maybe this was something I had to do on my own. I still hadn't given Kate an answer when the sergeant chipped in.

"If you could stay, Ms George. DC Travis has some questions for you."

CHAPTER TWENTY-ONE

Kate and the detective looked at one another, saying nothing until they heard the door shut, as if waiting for a signal that the two men had gone.

"Sorry, but I need the loo," said Kate, getting up and going upstairs.

As she went in the bathroom, the rhythm of *Lovers in a Dangerous Time*, the last song she and Sam had listened to, pulsed through her mind. She knew what the confident young constable was up to. Before they arrived, she and Penrose would have planned to separate Sam and Kate in the hope she would give something away without meaning to. Sam would be a prime suspect, no doubt about that. One didn't need to be in the police to know about all the women killed by their partners and ex-partners.

She began to wash her hands, determined to take her time over it. She didn't want to go back downstairs until she was ready. As she rubbed soap into her hands, she wondered how Michelle was, remembering her friend's tearful farewell at Lovendale airport a few days after Dawn's funeral. She'd been catching the flight to Amsterdam, then a connection from Schiphol to JFK. A part of Kate envied her for being so far away; another part longed for her to come back and help her through this. She berated herself for selfishness. Michelle would still be grieving.

As soon as Kate returned, DC Travis began her questioning.

"Are you feeling OK?"

"Yes, shocked of course, but..."

"Only natural. It's difficult to think straight at a time like this, but it's important we get as much information as possible as soon as we can."

Travis had a strong local accent and gave the impression of being everyone's friend. One could imagine her on a night out, a big smile on her face, one of the girls without a care in the world. She was using the force of her personality to put Kate at ease.

"I understand."

Kate steeled herself for whatever was coming next.

"I understand this house belongs to a Michelle Thomas and you're kind of looking after it at the minute," said DC Travis. "When I heard about that I thought, well, that's different. How did it come about exactly?"

"Michelle had a job lined up in New York and needed a house- sitter. I had decided to give up my job, so…"

"Something must have triggered it."

"To be honest, I wanted to get away from my rat of a husband and his pregnant lover. I had no wish to see the proud father wheeling a pushchair across Kew Green."

"Understandable. You were a police officer, weren't you?"

"I was a detective inspector in the Metropolitan Police."

The DC nodded and looked thoughtful for a moment.

"So you gave up a secure job and moved up here to be with Mr Flint?"

"No. I only met him a few weeks ago."

"So your relationship with Sam is not long-term?"

"I hadn't even seen Sam until I arrived in Alderton to move into this house. As you've probably gathered, we were attracted to each other. Today was the first time we'd done anything about it."

"I thought you might have met when you were visiting Michelle."

"No, I'd never been here before I moved in at the end of May."

Michelle had invited her to come and stay often enough. Why hadn't she accepted? It hardly mattered now.

"One thing does puzzle me, Kate. When Sergeant Penrose spoke to Mr Flint about Tiffany Booth's death, he denied you were his girlfriend."

"As I have already explained, Constable, we only met a short time ago."

The DC looked unconvinced.

"Have you met Sam's wife?"

"No."

"What did Sam say about her?"

"Nothing much. He was hardly going to talk about his wife if he was..."

"Chatting you up?"

"Well, yes. I mean, I haven't told Sam about my husband either."

"Now, you say he came round this evening. How did he seem when he got here?"

Kate shrugged.

"OK. The same as always, bearing in mind I'd only met him a handful of times."

"He wasn't upset or flustered?"

She shook her head.

"Would you say Mr Flint was bitter about the break-up of his marriage?"

"You're asking the wrong person, detective. As I said, I didn't know anything about it."

When DC Travis had gone, Kate thought back to the home she had lived in with Charles. Sold now, the proceeds shared. The end of a part of her life that was meant to go on forever. Till death us do part and all that stuff. Now there was another man in her life, or would have been.

Did this have to happen at this precise time? The chance of any kind of relationship developing now seemed remote, to say the least. Not now every aspect of Sam's life, perhaps hers too, would be dissected before this investigation was over.

She really didn't need this. Should she go back to London, stay with Mummy and Daddy while she looked for a place of her own? Put the whole thing down to experience?

Again she thought of Sam, wondering how he was. Had the death of his wife obliterated from his memory the few minutes they had spent in bed together? Still, somebody had died. She shouldn't be thinking about sex, should she?

Travis and Penrose would go to great pains to prove Kate had met Sam before she came to house-sit. Her police background gave her some insight into the thinking behind the investigation. That was no help at all.

CHAPTER TWENTY-TWO

I stared numbly at the pale blue walls of the police interview room. I'd spent Saturday nights in better places, that was for sure. My mind kept taking me back to the mortuary where I'd had to identify Nadia's body. I couldn't get rid of the image of her lifeless face, a parody of the real person she had once been. I'd never forget the contusions around her neck, like the ones I'd seen on Tiffany's.

"Now, Mr Flint," said Sergeant Penrose. "You've been through your movements for today. Is there anything you haven't told me?"

"No."

"You didn't go to the flat at 17 The Green today?"

"Not today, no."

He let the silence build. That didn't faze me. Sitting in a room without speaking was no hardship.

"When was the last time you went there?"

"That would have been yesterday when Richard Keppler arrived. I took him along to the apartment, showed him where everything was, you know..."

Even saying that much was hard work.

"What do you know about Mr Keppler?"

Leaning forward, I put my elbows on the table and stared at a tea stain.

"Not much. He's a writer apparently. Up here to finish a novel... look, Sergeant, I don't see what this has to do with..."

"It seems Mr Keppler met your wife at a Labour Party function in Manchester, where he lives."

"What?"

"You didn't know that?"

"No, I didn't."

I took a deep breath then slumped back in my chair. How did this friend of Nadia's come to be staying in a flat belonging to me?

"You'd better explain," I said.

"Mr Keppler was having an affair with your wife. They wanted to keep it quiet because he is married."

This new information should have been a shock but all I felt was confusion. I had been finding out stuff about her since the day we were married. One more thing hardly mattered now.

"Nadia recommended the apartment to Richard Keppler so they would have somewhere to meet. Mr Keppler says he had no idea the owner was Nadia's husband."

My name would have meant nothing to him: Nadia kept the name Harding when we got married. I could imagine her gloating at the thought of being with her lover in my flat.

"Did he know Nadia was married?"

"No, but he did know about her relationship with Olivia."

"I presume Olivia knows Nadia's dead?"

"Yes. She's very distressed."

She would be; she'd loved Nadia. I had loved her once. Pity Nadia had been a pain in the bum for much of our married life. I thought of all we'd been through together. After I'd supported her through some terrible times what was the point of walking out like she did? Too late for regrets now. Maybe she was at peace at last. She certainly never was when she was alive. I'd almost switched off from the police questioning but there was no escape.

"How did your daughter get on with her mother?"

"She didn't. I take it you know the background."

Penrose shook his head.

"Did you know Nadia was an alcoholic?"

"So Mr Keppler said but he knew nothing about it until your daughter told him."

"Emily told him?"

"According to Mr Keppler, your daughter went to the flat to see if Mr Keppler was satisfied with the accommodation. She found her mother there with him; there was an angry exchange."

Course there was. Angry exchanges were all we had left. As far as the police were concerned this must be one more complication.

"Listen, there's a history to this," I said, "you're gonna find out sooner or later so I'll tell you myself."

This was just the beginning. There would be much worse to come.

"When I met Nadia, I suppose she drank quite a bit," I began, "but so did I. We were young. But when she found out she was pregnant, she stopped just like that. Until Emily was around fifteen months."

"What happened then?"

Now I'd have to drag up memories I would just as soon have forgotten.

"I went to London to stay with a mate. Saturday morning to Monday morning I was away. We went to the test match at Lord's."

"So you left your wife on her own with a young child?"

I'd been on this guilt trip several times; I wasn't going to do it again.

"No, it wasn't like that..."

"What was it like then?"

Stay calm, I told myself.

"Nadia's university friend, Tessa, was coming to stay with her."

I could have told him that I'd looked after Emily while Nadia went away to Open University summer school a month previously but this wasn't about me justifying myself.

"Go on, Mr Flint."

"Anyway, Tessa phoned to cancel about an hour after I left so, as it turned out, Nadia and Emily were on their own."

I'd never liked that Tessa. She felt sorry for us because we lived in the North, kept telling us to move to Royal Berkshire, and live with the elite.

"I texted Nadia a few times while I was away. She texted back about days out they'd had. She didn't tell me Tessa hadn't turned up."

"Go on," said the sergeant when I stalled for a few seconds.

"As the train back to Loventon pulled in, I was looking forward to seeing Nadia and Emily. I thought I'd check my phone for messages, but I hadn't turned it on. It had been a rush to get away in time. There was a voice mail message to phone Dave Mawson at Social Services."

"What did you do?"

"Phoned him of course. He said there'd been a bit of a problem – he would come straight round to the house to explain and would be there by the time I got home."

I remembered jumping into a taxi and urging the driver to get a move on. The sick taste in my throat and the tension in my gut came back as if it were all happening again.

"When I got in, there were two empty vodka bottles on the living room carpet plus a few Carlsberg full strength cans. It looked like there had been a wild party but Nadia wasn't the wild party type and she couldn't stand mess."

"Quite a shock."

You could say that.

"About five minutes later, there was a knock at the door. Dave Mawson."

He had a beard, that was what I noticed first. Stocky and muscular. Looked as if he played rugby.

"I was a bit bewildered by this time so I asked him to come in and sat him down. I even apologised for the mess but of course he'd already seen it. I asked him to explain."

"'Both Emily and Nadia are fine' he said. He told me the social services had had an anonymous call Sunday evening that Nadia was drunk in charge of Emily. I tried to argue but she'd been drinking more or less constantly for two days."

The confusion, sadness and anger came flooding back as I spoke. Fat tears ran down my cheeks.

"Emily was with foster carers in Bentley – the social worker agreed I could collect her and bring her home later that day. Nadia had stayed in hospital overnight."

In my head I replayed the scene where I saw Emily at the foster parents. She toddled up to me, a huge smile on her face. I picked her up and flung my arms round her. I'd never been so happy and relieved.

"What happened next?"

"Well... you have to understand this was only the start. We had to go to a meeting. Emily's name went on some sort of register for a while. Nadia didn't drink for a few months, Emily's name came off the register and I thought things were back to normal."

"But they weren't?"

"Not by a long way. Nadia would relapse, there'd be another crisis, more meetings, name back on the register. Anyway, when Emily was about three and a half, Nadia fell off the wagon yet again."

I sank back in my chair, uncertain whether I could go on with this. I managed somehow.

"That was it. Social Services wouldn't allow Emily to stay at home if Nadia was left in sole charge. I juggled my work commitments so I was at home more. My mam and dad rallied round – I can't tell you how much they have done for us."

"What about Nadia's family?"

"We never saw much of them. Nadia didn't get on with them. She hinted about problems, said she'd had a difficult childhood but never really opened up about it."

"So they weren't able to help?"

"Weren't willing more like. When Emily was about six months old, they moved back to New Zealand, where Nadia was born."

I stopped talking, suddenly unable to continue. Could I cope with this? I was gonna have to.

CHAPTER TWENTY-THREE

"Emily, I know this is a bad time," said DC Travis, "but I have to ask you some questions."

Emily puffed out her cheeks, closing her eyes for a second.

"Questions?"

Emily looked at Travis like a bewildered child.

"Yes. Can you tell me when you last saw your mother?"

"Emily? You OK?"

The DC looked at her with friendly concern.

"Yeah, I'm..."

She thought for a little longer.

"Today at Dad's holiday flat, that was the last time I saw Mum."

"Can you tell me what happened there?"

"Is there any point when you must know the answer? If Richard Keppler found Mum's body, he must have told the police about my visit to the flat."

"I need to hear it in your own words."

With a supreme effort Emily switched off her emotions and, like a machine, told DC Travis about seeing her mum with Keppler, the row they had, the author's bewilderment. Sticking to facts was a comfort somehow.

"Why did you go round to the flat?"

"To see if everything was OK."

"Sorry?"

"It's my job to clean the flats, get them ready for occupation; I visit the guests to make sure they have everything they need."

"You're sure you didn't pop round in the hope of catching them together?"

"No way."

"I guess you were very angry about the way your mother behaved?"

"How did you work that out? I could be a detective."

"If you could just answer the question."

"There's a long history and you probably know all about it so I won't pretend everything was, like, perfect. Mum was an alcoholic and, well, I ended up in care a couple of times, I was on the at risk register or whatever you call it. Oh, God."

"You OK?"

She leaned forward in her seat.

"Of course, I'm not OK. I'm knackered apart from anything else. And you've just told me my mum's been murdered… I don't want to go on with this."

She took her glasses off and put them on again. After half a minute of silence, Emily spoke again.

"I suppose there's no escape. Go on with your questions."

"What you said about the alcoholism, having to go into care and everything. That's enough to make anyone bitter."

"Some of my friends, right, they say they want to be different, but I know they don't. Everybody wants to be like everyone else, normal. Mainstream. With me it's like… it's kind of a longing deep down inside of me."

Again, she stopped speaking.

"Go on."

"It's… I mean, it's… sorry, I can't put it into words…"

"Can you say how you feel about your mother's death?"

"Shocked, upset."

"Where did you go after you'd been to the holiday flat?"

"We're back to facts, that's good. I can handle them better than emotions."

Emily put her hand up to her face and discovered her cheeks were wet.

"After you left the flat?" the detective constable reminded her.

"I came home."

"And?"

"Mooched around, did some washing, read Harry Potter. I was a bit... on edge, you know, restless."

Neither of them spoke for a while.

"You didn't go back to the apartment?"

"Not really."

Travis had been busy writing since she'd started her interrogation, recording everything for posterity.

"Where did you go?"

She shrugged.

"Through the village. In the general direction of the flat, I guess you could say."

More silence. Emily averted her eyes, twiddled with the bracelet on her wrist, glanced at her watch without noticing what time it was.

"We have located a witness who saw you at the flat just after five o'clock."

Emily breathed evenly for a moment, placing her hands on her knees.

"I didn't go in the flat. I went near it."

"Near it?"

Emily nodded.

"You were seen looking in the window at the back."

"Really?"

"Yes. Why were you there, Emily?"

"I, er, wanted to talk to Mum, you know, kind of clear the air."

"Clear the air?"

"Yes, talk things over. Anyway, I never got to talk to her. I could see through the window she was asleep in an armchair. Drunk, I thought. So I walked away."

"Was there anybody else about."

"There was someone running along the footpath. Wearing a red hoody, going like the clappers."

"Do you know who it was?"

She shook her head.

"Too far away."

"Well, that's all for now," said Lindsey Travis.

For now? What did that mean?

"Although we shall require you to have your fingerprints taken."

* * *

Had she given too much away? That was Emily's first thought when the DC had gone. She could have said much more about her feelings but 'I don't believe my mum loved me' was something she could only say in her head, not to a police officer who suspected her of murder. The words of Bev, her therapist, came back to her. Something about having to come to terms with her mother's imperfections. Imperfections? A good way of putting it. The trouble was Mum loved people en masse, took up causes, but on an individual level, no chance.

How *did* Emily feel now her mum was dead? To ninety-nine point nine percent of the population the answer to that question would have been clear. There'd been times when the rejection hurt Emily so much she began to wish her mother was dead. Detective Constable Travis didn't need to know that. She was investigating a murder, finding out whodunnit. That had to be somebody with a motive; someone who knew her; a family member perhaps. A rejected daughter for instance.

The game of cat and mouse would presumably continue until Lindsey Travis was satisfied, couldn't think of any more questions or ran out of steam, whichever came first. Emily felt as if this would go on forever. Mum was dead but she was still haunting her. Why couldn't she have staggered drunkenly in front of a bus instead of getting herself murdered?

CHAPTER TWENTY-FOUR

The man standing on the doorstep the next morning just after eight o'clock had slumped shoulders, the remains of a black eye and an expression of exhausted gloom on his face. That made two of us who had lost a night's sleep.

"Hi, Sam. I just thought I would come round and...," he said.

And what? See how I was? Well, I felt and probably looked like death warmed up. I'd crawled out of bed at half seven and got dressed, telling myself I'd have a shower later. Why was Richard Keppler visiting me? I opened the door wider and let him in, leading the way into the kitchen, where we sat at the table.

"The thing is, Sam, I just wanted to talk about Nadia, you know."

Was he expecting a cosy chat, an exchange of anecdotes, an insight into what Nadia was like when she was younger?

"Listen, Richard. Nadia and me haven't been together for a while now. What she did was none of my business. I'm sorry she's dead, more sorry than I can say, but..."

He leant his elbows on the table, rubbing his chin nervously.

"Me too. I guess I'm in shock or something, not sure what I'm doing. Finding her like that, the police questioning me, it's the kind of thing I write about. The real thing's different."

Like I didn't know that.

"After Emily had left the flat, Nadia and I had a stand-up row. About, you know, stuff she hadn't told me. I had no idea she had a daughter, she never said anything about the drink problem."

He turned to face me as if expecting sympathy. He could forget that. I breathed heavily through my mouth, tapping my fingers on the table top. He went on.

"After a while she stormed out. I tried to do some work on my book but I couldn't concentrate. About, I dunno, four o'clock or so, Nadia came back."

"What did she want?"

He shrugged.

"To talk things over, she said. She was very contrite and... anyway, I let her in."

I'd been through something similar myself many times. She was forever pleading for one more chance.

"We chatted for a while without reaching any sort of conclusion. After half an hour or so I went out to get some milk. That was just an excuse, I needed time to think. When I returned, Nadia was lying dead in the armchair."

Richard turned towards me. I noticed fading bruising round his eye.

"How did you get the black eye, by the way?"

Richard averted his gaze.

"Black eye?"

He tried to inject surprise in his voice but it didn't fool me.

"Yeah. Nadia's handiwork, I take it. Join the club."

"Don't know what you're talking about."

He sounded too much like a petulant teenager to be convincing.

"What's this? Not speaking ill of the dead? Embarrassment? Shame?"

He gripped the edge of the table and looked from side to side.

"All three," he confessed. "It's kind of hard to be honest about it. It usually happens to women, doesn't it, domestic abuse or whatever they call it? People talk about it more these days. Is it somehow more of a taboo because it's a guy on the receiving end?"

"It's still wrong."

It had taken me years to understand that simple truth.

"I didn't realise she was an alcoholic, maybe I should have made allowances..."

"It's still wrong," I repeated, "I made allowances for years. God knows what it did to Emily, seeing and hearing things no child should ever be exposed to."

No point in regrets now.

"She's quite feisty, your daughter, she can look after herself, I'd say."

What the hell did he know about it?

"She's been doing that from an early age."

I'd been distracted by Nadia's problems, by the hope I would somehow sort her out if I only tried a bit harder. As long as Nadia was the centre of attention, nobody else mattered. The trouble was I'd been drawn into that and had ended up neglecting my own daughter.

"Sounds like you're blaming yourself. None of this is your fault, mate."

Nadia's death certainly wasn't my fault. I was a suspect though. So was Richard Keppler. We both had reason to kill her; at least I had someone to share that burden with. What did we do now? Crack open a bottle of whisky and have a bonding session? To hell with that.

"Look, Richard, no offence, but I'd like you to leave now."

He shrugged and got up.

"Oh, Richard," I said, "just one thing. When you'd just arrived in the village, you said something like, 'if anybody asks about me, you haven't seen me'. What did you mean?"

"I guess I was trying to make sure nobody saw me with Nadia."

After he'd gone, I wondered whether that was really true. Then I curled up on the settee and went to sleep.

CHAPTER TWENTY-FIVE

Around noon the day after Nadia's death, Kate went round to Sam's house and after a momentary hesitation, rang the bell. She had slept surprisingly well, then spent most of the morning asking herself questions about Sam. Would he want to see her? Would he be too tired, stressed, upset to see anyone? If she didn't call round, would he think she didn't care?

It was the last question that decided her. She did care. The poor man must be physically and emotionally shattered. Of course she should go and see him. When he opened the door, he stared vacantly at her for several seconds. His eyes only stayed open with a great effort. The same check shirt he'd worn the previous day was creased and not too clean. His lovely fair hair was greasy. He looked as though he'd shrunk overnight.

"Hi," she said, doing her best to sound cheerful. "I thought I'd come and see how you are."

He blinked his eyes as though coming round from an anaesthetic and rubbed the stubble on his chin.

"If it's, you know, not convenient..."

Her words tailed off.

"Oh, it's you, Kate. Sorry, I'm all over the place at the minute. Come in."

In the living room she sat on the settee, but Sam remained standing. He looked in the mirror on the wall.

"Look at the state of me."

He tried to tidy his hair.

"Tell you what, Kate. If you don't mind, I'll go and have a quick shower. Make myself presentable. I'll... er, see you in a few minutes, all right?"

"OK."

* * *

"I'm in the kitchen," she called when she heard Sam coming downstairs.

"I thought you might like a coffee," she said as he came in.

He'd changed into a blue shirt and smart grey trousers.

"Great, you must be a mind reader."

He sat opposite her at the table, while she poured the coffee.

"How are you?" she asked. "You look a bit..."

Sam smiled ruefully.

"Knackered?"

She smiled back.

"More than that and no wonder. Where's Emily?"

"She's still in bed. I thought I'd let her sleep. We were up late talking things over."

"Right."

"We were both questioned by the police for quite a while... it was like, God I don't know what it was like... Anyway, it's nice of you to call round, sorry if I was a bit strange when you arrived."

"You have a right to be as strange as you like. You've had a tough time. How did things go with the police?"

He poured more milk in his coffee and stirred it slowly.

"As you'd expect, I suppose. Or possibly not. I've been finding out... oh, lots of things…"

He breathed in and out twice as if following a ritual.

"Nadia was having an affair with Richard Keppler, the guy who discovered her body."

"God."

"I'd better fill you in on the family background, Kate."

Sam went through Nadia's drink problem, Emily being taken into care and Nadia eventually leaving.

"Oh, my God, Sam. It must have been terrible."

"Yeah, and now this. It's all a bit of a shambles, isn't it?" said Sam. "You realise I'm a suspect for Nadia's murder? So is Emily. It will be hanging over us for, well, forever."

"Sam..."

"Unless they find out who really did it. And they haven't had much success with the other two murders, have they?"

"Don't worry, they will," said Kate, sounding more confident than she felt.

"But there's a lot of unsolved murders out there, aren't there?"

She nodded.

"Listen, Kate, this might not be the right time, but... oh, hell, I'm just wondering whether we might spend a bit of time together once all this is..."

"I'd like that."

"If you decided all this mess makes it impossible, I'd understand."

She shook her head.

"No, not at all. To be boringly practical I'll have to go soon. I'm booked on the 3.30 train to London and haven't even packed."

"Oh, you're off to see your mam and dad, I'd forgotten about that. I'll give you a lift to the station."

"Thanks."

"Hey, when you get to London, don't be telling everybody how nice it is up here, will you?"

"What?"

"We don't want to be overrun by southerners. Not that I've got owt against them, it's just a question of numbers."

"I suppose some of your best friends are from the south."

"Only you so far."

"That's all right then."

CHAPTER TWENTY-SIX

After Kate left, I wondered whether to wake Emily, but decided against it. I was just wondering how I could keep an eye on her over the next few days without making it too obvious, when somebody knocked on the door. I thought of not answering but it could have been the police.

"Sam, can we talk?"

Olivia Brent.

"Sam, please?"

"Come in."

Was I to entertain all Nadia's lovers, male and female? That would take a while. In the living room, Olivia positioned herself in an armchair as though she'd been practising how to sit down elegantly. She was a striking woman. Not conventionally good-looking, but her Italian background gave her an exotic look. You had to look more closely to see the tiredness around her eyes carefully concealed with make-up. She rearranged her short, dark hair and pulled down the hem of her blue T-shirt. Even at a time like this, she had to look her best.

"I had no idea about her and Keppler, did you?"

I shook my head. She played with her silver necklace then put her hands on her lap.

"How could she? We were going to get married as soon as the divorce was finalised. We'd talked about adoption."

Adoption? Nadia wouldn't have got past the first interview. Nadia Harding? Not the alcoholic who almost ruined her own child's life? We're not letting her near another kid. Did Olivia even know about all that? I could imagine Nadia covering it up.

"Anyway, I really came round to talk about the funeral."

When she'd phoned earlier asking for 'thoughts about the funeral' I told her I would get back to her in a couple of days. Not good enough for Olivia. What she wanted, she had to have. Now.

"Yeah?"

"I was wondering if you could organise it. I don't think I could cope. I'll pay of course."

Poor you. What if I said I couldn't cope? Before I could respond, she went on.

"Oh, I know what you think of me. Poor little rich girl. Spoilt rotten. Always gets what she wants."

This was so near to my true feelings, there was no point in polite denials.

"Well, that's not true. It was Nadia who insisted we move in together. I tried to say no, told her how it would hurt you and Emily. But in the end, I just couldn't help myself."

Course you couldn't, Olivia.

"I'll arrange the funeral, but we'll have to wait for the police to finish whatever they have to do."

"Oh, thank you, Sam."

After the briefest of goodbyes, she left.

* * *

Three days later at about six o'clock in the evening I watched Kate wheeling her suitcase into the car park of Loventon station. Seeing me standing by the van, she smiled and waved. That didn't mean a thing. Once she had put a couple of hundred miles between us, I'd bet any amount of money that the reality of the murder had hit her. Then she'd be having second thoughts about a bloke in my position. She strolled towards me in that way she had, as if she had all the time in the world. When she reached me, she gave me a big hug.

"Well, you're a sight for sore eyes," she said.

"So are you."

Did this mean everything would be all right?

"It's so good to be back," she said as we got under way. "London's so crowded and noisy."

I smiled at the idea of Kate echoing my thoughts.

"And Daddy was at his worst."

Kate went on at some length about her controlling father. All light-hearted and jokey.

"Is there any news?" she asked as we reached the outskirts of Alderton.

"Not much. The police haven't made a breakthrough, but we can go ahead with the funeral. It'll be next Monday, the fifth of July."

She nodded.

"Not working today?" she asked as we pulled up in Loven Terrace.

I looked over towards her.

"No, I'm having a few days off."

"Do you, er, have any plans?"

I reached out and took her hand.

"I thought we could maybe do something."

* * *

"Well, we've done something," said Kate later.

We snuggled together in her bed.

"Yeah," I grinned. "One of my better ideas."

"Yes. We must do it again sometime."

I kissed her.

"Let me get my breath back."

CHAPTER TWENTY-SEVEN

Just after Sam had left, Kate got a call from Michelle.

"I'm in Edinburgh," she said.

"Edinburgh?"

"Yes, it's to do with work. Flying visit, last minute job. I'm going back in two days' time so I thought I might come and see you tomorrow. I'm booked on the 9.45 train."

"Great."

"Any news?"

"Quite a bit actually, but I'll tell you tomorrow."

Kate could do with a friend to talk to.

* * *

"I'm stunned," said Michelle the following day at the kitchen table.

Kate had brought her up to date about recent happenings over lunch. Michelle took a swig of the Californian Merlot she had brought with her, then finished off her chicken salad.

"You know about these things, Kate. What do you think's going on?"

"I'd say it's likely that Dawn, Tiffany and Nadia were killed by the same person."

"That makes sense."

Both women fell silent for a while, until Kate asked a question.

"Michelle, what was Nadia like?"

Michelle twiddled the stem of her glass and watched the wine swirl around.

"Nobody knew what she was like. It was as if she was trying to build up an image for herself... oh, it's hard to explain but anybody who came across her would say the same."

Kate had been looking for a straight answer but it seemed she was going to get something more complex.

"You see, Kate, it was all put on with Nadia."

"How do you mean?"

"Well, for example, when somebody told me she was bi-sexual, I thought 'she would be'."

"That's a bit homophobic, isn't it?"

She shook her head.

"No, Nadiaphobic maybe. God, she was so up herself. Silly, affected bitch. Tried everything to find herself. Vegetarianism, Buddhism, meditation. Why not add lesbianism to the mix."

"Right."

"There was nothing natural about her. Anything for effect, that was Nadia," she said, the hint of a sneer in her voice. "It was her work on the council more recently. She liked all the wheeler-dealing that goes on behind the scenes. And it's a chance to be the centre of attention."

Michelle stopped for breath.

"You didn't like her much, did you?" asked Kate.

"How did you guess? I haven't even got onto the way she treated Sam and Emily yet."

"I know something about that."

Michelle looked puzzled for a moment.

"Why are you so interested, Kate?"

Kate replied with an adolescent shrug.

"Oh, you know..."

Michelle gave her what her mother would have called an old-fashioned look.

"Come on, Kate. I know you. What aren't you telling me?"

"Well, Sam and I have become quite friendly of late..."

"Friendly?"

Kate nodded.

"You mean you're shagging him?"

"Yes."

Michelle's grin lit up her face.

"You lucky thing. So there is some good news, eh? How did it all start?"

"Well, we got into bed and..."

Michelle grinned again. Kate was glad to have cheered her friend up.

"I'll take that as read. What led up to it more, you know... generally?"

Kate explained about their snog on the river bank and the police arriving to announce Nadia's murder and what followed.

"Oh, my God," said Michelle. "You wanted a change and you've certainly got one. But, I mean, what are you going to do long-term?"

"I'm no more able to answer that question now than I was when I got here."

Suddenly serious, the two women sat in uncomfortable silence for a while.

"You don't have to stay here, you know," Michelle said.

"I do."

"Of course you don't, Kate. You can get in your car this minute and drive off into the sunset. Get back into London life, get your old job back..."

Kate shook her head vehemently.

"No. No."

"You could have the occasional holiday in New York. I could show you the Big Apple..."

"The New York bit sounds great, but I have to stop running away from things. That's what I do every time anything goes wrong."

"That's not true, Kate."

"Yes, it is. Me and my smug, little life. I sailed through school, always strong and successful, always in control. I was head girl, captain of the cricket team, you name it. There had never been any hint of failure… Sorry, I seem to be in confessional mode lately."

Michelle took her hand.

"Oh, Kate."

"I know it's going to be tough being put through a murder inquiry, but I'll cope."

"Will you though?"

"I think I can help Sam through it. Perhaps what I'm getting at is I can't just walk away at the first sign of trouble."

"Good luck."

"We'll probably need it. As Nadia's husband, Sam will be a suspect. Goes without saying."

"She was pretty awful to him."

"I realise that, but I keep coming back to the simple fact that three people have been killed in a small village. The same person must have murdered them. It doesn't make sense otherwise. So, it's either a serial killer – and they're not as common as you might think – or someone has a strong motive connected with all three women. Someone with a lot to lose."

"But who? And what? Dawn, Tiffany and Nadia weren't friends or anything."

Kate pondered what her friend had said before replying.

"But they did have things in common. They knew one another, they were all women, they lived near one another."

Kate saw a sadness in her friend's face.

"I'm sorry, Michelle, if you don't want to talk about all this, we'll change the subject."

"I don't *want* to talk about it but feel I must. If what happened to the other two has a bearing on my sister's death, I need to know about them."

CHAPTER TWENTY-EIGHT

Mark sat in Emily's back yard after her mam's funeral. Emily's Dad was with a woman Mark had never met before. Kate, they called her. Her and Sam Flint were an item apparently. Nice one, Sam. Who'd have believed he'd manage to pull someone like Kate? She was obviously from down south, well-to-do background at a guess. She was the type he went for himself, older with a touch of class.

This was the first funeral he'd ever been to and he didn't want to go to any more. The constant reminders of death had started to do his head in by the time they got out of the church. He was too young to think about things like that. The ceremony was, he reckoned, like any other, though not many had the police in attendance. The detective who'd questioned him in the garden of the Bricklayers sat at the back. Mark couldn't see the point of her being there. What would she learn from listening to Clive Wheatley droning on?

Mark had learnt a lot more about Emily's family since her mam had died. That Miss Brent, the teacher he'd met in the Castlebridge shop, was Nadia's 'partner'. Her mother was bi-sexual in other words and had even been having an affair with a guy at the time she died. And that wasn't all. She'd had a problem with the booze and couldn't look after her daughter properly. Emily had always said she was a bit weird. What an understatement.

Still, it meant Emily was opening up to him, kind of relying on him to give emotional support. He never imagined she would want him at the funeral but she insisted she needed him by her side. She certainly needed somebody. He'd never seen anybody so chewed up. The cops harassing her didn't exactly help. All these thoughts had time to pass through his mind as they sat there. He was surprised when Kate broke the gloomy silence that surrounded them.

"Now that the funeral is over perhaps you can get back to normal."

Sam loosened his tie before speaking.

"You know, Kate, I don't think we'll ever get back to normal."

Kate took his hand.

"Oh, Sam."

"To put it bluntly," said Sam, "DS Penrose thinks either me or Emily killed Nadia. They've been hounding us since Nadia's body was found. We'll never have any peace until the case is solved."

Kate looked over to Emily, a look of concern on her face.

"I'm going for a walk," said Sam, getting up, "anybody coming?"

Kate got to her feet.

"I'll join you."

Mark looked at Emily, who spoke for both of them.

"We're OK, thanks."

"Don't worry, Sam, I'll look after her," said Mark.

Sam nodded. Mark put his hand in Emily's. When the other two had gone, Emily turned to Mark and kissed him. Tears streamed down her face.

"I couldn't have faced this without you. Thanks for coming, Mark."

"No probs. Least I could do."

Mark looked into the future and saw Emily and him battling through more tough times. Was that what they meant by 'for better, for worse'?

"We'll get through it together."

They stood up and walked into the house. The front door bell rang almost as soon as they got there. When they went to answer it, Mark recognised DC Travis. A man was by her side. They both had ID cards ready.

"Emily Flint," he said.

"Yes."

"I'm DS Penrose, Lovendale police, this is Detective Constable Travis..."

"I know who she is. Come in."

In the living room the officers turned down the offer of a seat. DS Penrose was the first to speak.

"Emily Flint, I am arresting you for the murder of Nadia Jane Harding. You do not have to say anything but..."

As the sergeant recited the formal caution, Emily and Mark stared at one another, at a loss for words.

"You can't do this, you've got it all wrong," said Mark, finding his voice.

"If you could just let us do our job, Mr Hanwell."

Emily laid her hand gently on his arm, as if he were the one who was in need of reassurance.

"It's OK, Mark. It's just a mistake, we'll sort it out. You just wait here for Dad and tell him what happened."

She kissed him then turned to Penrose.

"Ready when you are."

Mark watched them go, then closed the door. He wasn't expecting that, but there was no point in worrying about it. Now was the time for action. If there was one thing he had learned from his less than perfect family, it was what to do when someone was arrested. He got out his phone and turned to his contacts. Seconds later he was talking to a solicitor.

"Zoe," he said, "Mark Hanwell here."

"Hi, what can I do for you?"

"My girlfriend's in a bit of bother. Arrested for murder."

"That sounds like a lot of bother. Better give me a few details."

He explained what had happened.

"Right," said Zoe, "I'll get to the police station straight away."

He went into the living room again and waited. It was half an hour before he heard the front door open. Kate and Sam walked in, looked around the room and sat down.

"Where's Emily?" asked Sam.

Mark took a deep breath.

"The cops came round half an hour ago. They've taken her to the station. She's been arrested for her mam's murder."

"What?"

Sam leapt up.

"No! They can't do that. Why didn't you stop them?"

"Stop them? How could I?"

"It's not Mark's fault, Sam," Kate said.

Sam paced the room, anger distorting his face.

"I know, sorry, Mark."

"No probs, mate. I've got her a lawyer, by the way. Zoe Troble, one of the best, she'll be with Emily now."

Sam stopped pacing and sat down.

"God. Is there nothing we can do?"

Kate took his hand.

"Of course there is. Mark has done the right thing, making sure she has legal representation."

"Thanks, Mark."

He even sounded as if he meant it.

"Will we be allowed to see her?" asked Sam.

"It's hard to say," said Kate. "We can go over there and see what's going on."

CHAPTER TWENTY-NINE

Emily faced a solicitor called Zoe, who was holding a large notebook in one hand, a biro in the other. She had never met this woman before and they were in a police interview room. Proof positive that the world had gone mad.

"Now then, Emily," said the lawyer, "I'll just explain a few things before we start. You're entitled to have me with you while you are interviewed."

"Right."

"Of course, as soon as I got here, I insisted on taking instructions from my client before the police can talk to you."

Zoe had nicotine-stained fingers, chewed nails and a suit that had seen better days. Judging by the bags under her eyes, the legal representative had also seen better days. How old was she, Emily wondered? Fiftyish? Older? Younger?

"Your client? Is that me?"

"I'm afraid so, honey. I need to get some facts straight. First off, why do you think the police think you killed your mother?"

She went through the family history of the Flints right up to the day her mother died.

"I see. Did you kill your mother?"

"No, I did not."

The effrontery of the question gave her renewed energy.

"Good. I had to ask."

"Yeah, sure."

"When we get in there it will be hard. I'll be there to help you. If you're stuck for an answer, just look at me and I'll jump in. You don't have to say a word, remember. Think carefully before you speak."

"What about the other murders? Two other women have been killed in Alderton recently."

"I was just coming to that. Tell me what you know about them and, most importantly, where you were at the time they were killed."

* * *

After they had finished their discussion, Zoe and Emily were taken to another interview room, where they sat facing DS Penrose and DC Travis. Penrose switched on the tape and went through a kind of ritual, naming all those present. It was as if the recording machine was a person who had to be introduced to everyone.

"Emily, you told DC Travis on Saturday 26th June that you had a difficult relationship with your mother, Nadia Harding. Is that correct?"

She nodded.

"Please answer for the tape."

"Yes."

"On the day your mother died you had an altercation with her, did you not?"

"Altercation? If you mean a row, that's right. I told the detective constable all this."

Penrose shuffled his papers around and coughed quietly before replying.

"We need to go through it again."

"Fine."

"After this argument with your mother, what did you do?"

"Went home. Went out again about five o'clock."

He proceeded to ask the same questions Lindsey Travis had asked. Emily gave the same answers. Penrose still wasn't satisfied.

"You say you got as far as the front door of the holiday flat, looked through the front window and then left."

Emily shook her head vehemently.

"No, as I told DC Travis I went round the back, saw somebody running down the path away from the flat, then looked in the window and saw Mum. That's exactly what happened."

Zoe touched Emily's arm, then spoke.

"Sergeant, I'm concerned at what is either an attempt to distort what my client said to your junior colleague or an example of unforgivable inefficiency. Ms Flint is as keen as you to discover who killed her mother."

"Nice one, Zoe," Emily whispered.

"Let me tell you what I think happened," said Penrose, unfazed.

The four people around the table looked at each other, waiting for the sergeant's big moment.

"When you got home from the holiday flat where you saw Nadia with Richard Keppler, by your own admission you felt restless. After a while you went out to see your mother."

He paused to look at his notebook. He had a pseudo-dramatic delivery, investing his words with extra meaning.

"You found she was still in the flat. Your anger had been building up all this time."

He picked up a glass of water that he had left untouched until now. He drank, watching her over the rim of the glass.

"Seeing your mother drunk again, you let yourself into the flat."

"I did not, I left *because* Mum was drunk. When I saw Mum through the window, I couldn't wait to get away. I was in such a hurry I banged my handbag on the picnic table and loads of stuff dropped out."

He picked up a clear plastic bag and passed it to Emily.

"I am now passing exhibit one to the accused."

"I'd like you to look at what's inside the bag. Don't take it out."

It was a length of wire with wooden handles attached. He went onto the next question.

"Do you recognise this?"

"What is it?"

"Have you ever seen it before?"

She glanced to the left and made eye contact with Zoe.

"Just think, Emily, to the best of your knowledge have you seen it before?"

She recognised it from somewhere. But where?

"To the best of her knowledge," put in Travis, the first time she had spoken, "surely she must know whether she's seen it or not."

Zoe touched Emily's arm again.

"It is quite possible that Emily may have seen this object before but would not have remembered precisely where."

"I could have seen it," said Emily. "It looks vaguely familiar, that's all I can say."

"Sergeant," said Zoe, "I can't help wondering where this is leading. You seem to be ignoring the fact that two other women in the small village of Alderton have been unlawfully killed within a few weeks. Is my client supposed to have killed them too?"

"If you could allow me to continue."

He looked smug as if he had something up his sleeve.

"Emily, you say you're not sure whether you have seen this item before. Can you explain how your fingerprints were found on the wooden handles?"

Emily swallowed hard and gripped the edge of the table.

"No, I can't."

Zoe jumped in again.

"What is the significance of this?"

"This cheese wire was used to kill Nadia Harding. Further tests are being done to ascertain whether this is also the implement that killed Dawn Fraser and Tiffany Booth."

CHAPTER THIRTY

"Yes?" said Kate to the woman slouching tiredly on her doorstep.

"You Kate?"

"Yes."

"I'm Zoe Troble, Emily's solicitor. Is her Dad with you? If so, I'd like a word please."

"Come in."

In the lounge, Kate introduced Zoe to Mark and Sam. Since returning from the police station, where they weren't allowed to see Emily, they sat drinking tea and talked round the subject of Emily's arrest.

"Hiya, Mark, how are you?" said the solicitor as she sat on an armchair.

"I was OK until this happened."

"We'll have to see what we can do about it then, won't we?"

Zoe turned to Kate.

"While I get my papers in order and my arse into gear, I don't suppose there's any chance of a coffee is there, honey? Black, nice and strong."

Kate got up to get the coffee while Zoe pulled notebooks and typed documents out of a cavernous bag.

"Oh, Kate, before you go, where's the bog?"

* * *

"Right," said Zoe later, after several swigs of coffee, "let's get started. First, some facts. Emily is to appear before magistrates in the morning. In the meantime, she is remanded in police custody."

"No!"

Sam's voice boomed through the room.

"Sorry, Sam, that's the way it is."

Sam slumped on the settee, shaking his head.

"The evidence against her looks strong on the face of it."

She went on to explain that Emily was seen very near the flat where her mother's body was found; her fingerprints were found on the handles of the cheese wire that had garrotted Nadia Harding; she could be said to have had a motive to kill her mother.

"At the minute," Zoe went on, "the charge is murdering Nadia Harding. At the time the others were killed, Emily's movements and whereabouts can be accounted for. That weakens their case."

"That's the whole point, surely the same person must have killed..." said Kate.

Zoe didn't let her finish.

"All three. Right. I reckon if they can't pin the other two crimes on Emily, they'll claim that as Emily knew the people who found the first two bodies, she also knew how the first two murders were committed."

"A copycat crime?"

"Precisely."

Sam joined the conversation.

"None of this makes any sense. Point number one: my daughter is not a murderer. Even the police concede she can't have done two of the murders. This copycat theory doesn't work because there's still the question of how she got hold of the murder weapon unless she did all three murders."

Mark chipped in.

"Can we go to court tomorrow, give her moral support, like?"

"Yes, the hearing's at half nine."

"We'll be there," said Sam.

Zoe steamrollered on.

"To build a proper defence, we need to know more about Tiffany Booth and Dawn Fraser. That's where you lot come in. I want you to think what you know about them. Emily told me something about Tiffany: she bought an iPhone 8 in the Avanatta shop and told Emily she had her little boy to thank for it. That suggests the child's father was paying for the phone – and other things – as the price for Tiffany keeping quiet about him."

Zoe's audience looked expectantly at her.

"Now, all of you, wrack your brains, talk it over between yourselves. Next time I see you, let me know what you come up with."

Kate, Mark and Sam looked helplessly at one another. Zoe turned to Kate.

"You're an ex-copper, aren't you? You can co-ordinate everything, OK? Take notes on this."

She took a small notebook from her bag and chucked it in Kate's direction. She caught it as if it were a straightforward slip catch. Zoe went on with her instructions.

"Anything that might conceivably help Emily, write it down. And I want it yesterday."

She drained her cup, packed her papers away and stood up.

"I'll see you in court."

* * *

After a few moments of stunned silence, Kate got things moving.

"Well, we've got our homework. Let's get started."

"What good can we do?" asked Sam. "This is gonna destroy Emily."

Kate turned to Sam.

"Sam, we have to find a way of helping her. That way perhaps it won't destroy her."

"You seem to forget her fingerprints were..."

"I know it's a stumbling block but only by being positive can we hope to get through this. All evidence can be challenged, even fingerprints. So-called experts can make mistakes just like anyone else."

"Yeah, course they can," agreed Mark.

"And even if the fingerprints do belong to Emily, there could be a logical explanation."

Sam looked far from convinced. A nervous twitch had started above his right eye.

"Right," she said with authority, "I think we should set about his thing systematically. Go through what we know about Dawn and Tiffany. I'll take notes and type them up for the solicitor."

"I'm not sure about this," said Sam.

"Well, I am," said Mark. "The way I see it, Sam, is this. Emily didn't kill her mam, right? The cops have got it wrong, simple as. Wouldn't be the first time, won't be the last. So they're missing summat. It's up to us to find it."

Kate gave Mark a look of encouragement.

"That makes sense to me. Sam?"

"Yeah. Worth a try, I suppose."

Mark was on a roll.

"The murders are connected. Course they are. They must be. I mean, it stands to reason, doesn't it? We've just got to find the link."

They all nodded.

"Right," he went on. "First question: what did the victims have in common? They all lived in Alderton."

Mark looked pensive for a moment then continued.

"Which means the murderer was probably from round here. He needed ease of access to the women he killed."

"Good point," said Kate, flashing him her nicest smile. "We need to look at the victims themselves in some detail. Personally, I think Dawn Fraser is the key. She had a string of lovers: we need to identify them."

Mark opened his mouth wide. Sam shook his head in disbelief.

* * *

When Sam and Mark had gone, Kate sat at the kitchen table with her laptop and notebook. Looking back on her discussion with the two men, she had been struck by their differing reactions. Sam was clearly amazed – particularly when he learned about Dawn's sexual adventures and her affair with his friend, Dale – but Mark's reaction was harder to work out. It was as though he were uneasy about something.

Both Sam and Mark had come up with useful information. Now it was her job to make sense of it. She had decided to type it up and send it to Zoe. She made a start, then read through what was on the screen.

VICTIMS

Dawn Fraser:
Dale Wilson was having an affair with Dawn. He was near her house at the relevant time. So was Paddy McCann, a notorious womaniser. She may have had a stalker. No idea who that could be, perhaps someone she met on holiday?

It seems she changed quite a lot after Ed left. Is that the key? Did she really see him in the Market Tavern a few days before she died? He stood to gain a lot of money from Dawn's death.

Tiffany Booth:
She had a child but refused to tell anybody the father's name. Why? Was the father married? Was she blackmailing him, making

him pay for her silence? She told Sam she 'knew things' about Paddy McCann. Was Tiffany one of Paddy's women?

She was having an affair with Brian from the shop. Was this serious? This could give Rebecca a motive. Where was she at the time of the murder? Was she really at work as she claims?

Nadia Harding:

She was an alcoholic from a troubled background. She left Sam for Olivia Brent but was also having a relationship with Richard Keppler. She had had a lot of extra-marital affairs. She had made changes in her life recently.

Kate thought about all this. Two things stood out. They all had several sexual partners. Did the killings arise out of some sort of religious belief that women shouldn't behave in this way? (Funny how these strictures never applied to men.) Or was it good old-fashioned jealousy because they were having sex with somebody's partner?

The other thing was they had all re-invented themselves in some way. After a life of great respectability, Dawn had 'shagged her way round the country' to quote her sister. Tiffany had started her own business. Nadia was forever re-inventing herself, most recently through getting herself elected as a councillor and her relationship with Olivia.

CHAPTER THIRTY-ONE

Two days later, as Mark drove to Alderton, where he was due to meet Kate in the cafe, Emily was on his mind as usual. Yesterday in court he had had to look on helplessly while she was remanded in custody. He only hoped they got Emily out of prison soon. He didn't like to think what being banged up was doing to her.

His reaction to his girlfriend's arrest and imprisonment had surprised him. Had it been anyone but Emily he would have run a mile. It would have been to his advantage to do that now, but he was going to stand by her and to hell with the consequences. Anybody who didn't like it knew what they could do.

It wouldn't do his prospects with Avanatta any good to be associated with Emily. When the redundancies started, he couldn't help thinking his name would be on the top of the list. The gaffer had hinted he should cut himself off from Emily, but there was no way he would do that. Instead, he would visit her as often as he could, tell anybody who would listen that she was innocent and do his best to support her dad.

* * *

Ten minutes later, Mark and Kate were having tea and scones in *Tea Time*. It was Mark's day off and he had come prepared, like Kate, with pen and notebook. It only took about ten minutes to share out key tasks between them and write a list. Kate's approach was carefully thought out. She had been as good as her word and wasted no time in knocking up a plan of action. Mark was impressed with her efficiency but most of all he was grateful.

"Sam still not wanting to get involved?" said Mark.

"That's right. I don't think he'd cope very well with any actual investigating."

"He's got enough on his plate as it is."

"How are things at work?" asked Kate.

"Not good. Emily Flint is bad for the Avanatta's image."

Before they could discuss any of this, Paddy McCann came in. He ordered a coffee at the counter and brought it over to their table. After Mark had introduced him to Kate, they fell silent. This was happening a lot lately. What did you say to a man whose girlfriend has been arrested for killing her mother?

"I heard about Emily," said Paddy eventually. "I'm really sorry, mate."

Mark nodded his thanks as the council leader went on.

"I can't believe it. It's got to be a mistake. I mean, it's..."

Kate explained her idea that could be summed up as: three murders, one murderer.

"If only we knew more, we'd be able to prove Emily's innocence," she said.

"Yeah."

"You know what's going on round here, Paddy," said Kate. "Could you tell us anything that might help?"

"I don't see how," said Paddy.

Kate was insistent.

"You might know something really important without realising it."

"That's what the police said when I spoke to them."

Kate and Mark exchanged a glance.

"You spoke to the police? When was this?"

He drank coffee and looked thoughtful for a while.

"Not long after Dawn Fraser was killed, I realised I was near Michelle's house on the day she died, so I went to see that Sergeant Penrose."

Kate sipped tea before asking her next question.

"What did you tell him?"

"Nothing much if I'm honest."

"What did you see?"

"Nothing significant."

Kate kept on with her questions.

"Did Penrose talk to you about the other murders?"

"He came to see me to ask about Tiffany. Apparently, I was playing golf at Bentley Hall around the time her body was found in the pavilion. I had no idea until Sergeant Penrose called."

"Could you help him, Paddy?" asked Mark.

"Sadly, no. In the case of Nadia, well, nobody thought it was worth talking to me."

Kate persevered.

"You knew the three women, didn't you? You might be able to give us a new insight."

"Suppose so but I wasn't friendly with any of them. I used to see Dawn around the village and say hello but I never exchanged more than a few words with her."

"What about the others?"

"Tiffany did a bit of painting for me but that was arranged through Sam. Nadia did my accounts once or twice. I've used Lumley and Finkle for years but it wasn't always Nadia who did the audit."

Kate tapped her teaspoon on the table in frustration.

"Come on, Paddy, think. You must know more than that. You're a big noise in the community, in charge of the council, director of Avanatta phone company. And you have a bit of a reputation with the ladies."

Kate was keeping it light but Mark heard the determination in her voice. Shock passed over Paddy's face to be quickly replaced by a sly grin.

"You're well informed, I'll give you that, but you shouldn't listen to rumours."

"I listen to little else. Let's cut to the chase. Have you had a dalliance with any of the three women who have been killed in Alderton recently?"

There was an alertness about all three of them as Paddy pondered his answer.

"So that's what you're getting at, is it? The answer to your question is none of your business."

He finished his coffee and got up.

"I'll have to love you and leave you, I'm afraid. I hope things work out OK."

Silence descended once more when he had gone.

"Sir Paddy wasn't much use," said Mark.

"*Sir* Paddy?"

"He soon will be by all accounts. For a while now there have been rumours he's due a knighthood next time the honours list comes out. He's already a CBE."

"Well, Rod Stewart's a sir, so anything is possible."

Mark smiled at the thought of calling Paddy McCann 'sir', then had a thought.

"If these rumours are true," he said, "Paddy would want to keep his nose clean until the knighthood is made official."

"So if anyone found out anything scandalous about him, he'd want it kept quiet."

* * *

Mark sat at the back of St Gregory's staring vacantly at the altar, ready to put into practice the plan he'd agreed with Kate a couple of days ago. It was, he supposed, a nice enough building if you were into that sort of thing but church architecture hadn't brought him here today. Nor had he come to church to pray. He had driven into Alderton in his lunch hour to call in on Clive Wheatley.

Now here he was waiting to talk to the vicar as part of the investigation. Kate thought it was vital to talk to Clive: he lived about three doors down from Michelle's house, where Dawn's body was found; he was an important person in the village; he and his wife would have known Dawn through church and Nadia as a neighbour. Tiffany occasionally took Harry to play with Jacob round at their place.

Mark had discussed with Kate about how he might approach Clive: what he was going to say, how he might lull him into a false sense of security; how he might get him to open up.

Kate had reckoned Clive would soon start to feel sorry for Mark. He would want to listen to a troubled, young man in the hope of convincing him that God was there for him always. When Clive found a way of introducing religion, Mark would have to pretend to take him seriously. At the same time, he'd be looking for a way to slip in a few questions that might get the answers he wanted, that might even include a bit of useful evidence. Could he pull it off?

* * *

After he had been waiting for twenty minutes Clive appeared, shuffling busily along the aisle. He carried a book and was in uniform.

"Clive," he said as the vicar rushed past without seeing him.

Clive looked round in confusion before his eyes lighted on Mark.

"Oh, hello."

"I was wanting a word if that's OK."

For a moment, the man of God hesitated.

"Of course, by all means."

The vicar sat beside Mark.

"We shouldn't be disturbed here," said Clive. "Now, what can I help you with?"

"It's about Emily."

The vicar nodded wisely.

"Yes, I rather thought it might be."

Mark was quiet for a moment, getting his thoughts together.

"To be honest, Clive, it's doing my head in."

"I can understand that, Mark."

"How can you understand, Clive? How can anyone? One person in a million, that's how many have been through what I'm going through."

"Mark…"

"She's stuck in a cell while we're sitting here. I really want to help her, know what I mean?"

Clive rubbed the palms of his hands together as if he were cold.

"She needs to know you're on her side, that you won't let her down..."

"I've gotta get her out of there, got to."

For a moment Clive looked shocked.

"Get her out…? You mean help her escape?"

"No, I want to prove she didn't do what she's accused of. She didn't do it, Clive. I mean, she wouldn't..."

"This may well be true, Mark, but that sort of thing is best left to the professionals. I think what you need right now is someone to talk to. I can fulfil that role if you so wish."

"The thing is, Clive, I reckon Tiffany, Dawn Fraser and Nadia Harding were killed by the same person. Does that make sense to you?"

"Possibly."

Mark might have known better than to expect a clergyman to commit himself.

"You must have known them all. What about Tiffany, what can you tell me about her?"

"Not much. I first met her when she came to paint the vicarage – it was her first job after she'd set up her little business. We hadn't been back in Alderton long."

Mark waited. He wasn't going to say any more. That way maybe Clive would feel obliged to say a bit more. After an awkward minute or so, it worked.

"Dawn I knew very well of course. She was very active in the church and the local community and a strong supporter of the Spiritual Renewal movement."

"Is that so? Sounds interesting."

"It's designed to help people to find ways of getting closer to God or overcoming any doubts they may be having."

"Right. How does that work then?"

This seemed to spark Clive's interest.

"Usually through group discussions, sometimes focused work with an individual."

"What's your role in this?"

"Well, Mark, sometimes I take part in groupwork as an equal member. I have conducted workshops and on occasion one-to-one sessions. Could, er, anything like this possibly help you?"

Mark nodded and set his face in a frown full of sincerity.

"It's certainly something I'd consider."

* * *

On his way home, he recalled what Clive had said about Dawn. So she was active in the local community, was she? That wasn't the only thing she was active in, thought Mark. He still hadn't got over hearing Dawn was shagging around. The sense of betrayal went deep, but you had to move on, didn't you? He would never get involved with anybody like that in future. No way. If he ever got Emily out of jail, he'd stick with her for good.

CHAPTER THIRTY-TWO

"Thanks for agreeing to see me, Dale," said Kate.

She knew Mark was carrying out his allotted task today so it was only right she should do her bit.

"No bother," said the reporter, wiping his oil-stained hands on a cloth. Kate had walked across the bridge opposite Michelle's house to reach Dale's parents' farm. Now she sat on a rickety chair in a dilapidated shed while he finished working on a huge, blue tractor.

"Working here must be quite a change from journalism."

"Yes, I'm glad to be outdoors and I like to help my mam and dad when I can. They've done a lot for me."

"Will you take over the farm eventually?"

He shrugged.

"Probably. I could never do it full-time though. At the minute I'm a bit of an odd-job man. I help with the harvest, repair fences and, like today, service tractors."

Kate looked across to the sheep roaming around fields. A peaceful rural scene, which made the idea of murder just yards away all the more unreal. Dale threw the cloth onto a workbench and sat on a hay bale.

"Right, I'm all yours. I'm guessing you've arranged this meeting to talk about Emily."

"That's right."

"It won't surprise you to know that neither Sam nor I believe Emily killed her mother. Nor does Mark, her boyfriend."

"Right."

"We are investigating the murders of Dawn Fraser, Tiffany Booth and Nadia Harding."

He looked surprised for a moment.

"All three of them? A tall order."

"Yes, but they're all connected."

Dale expressed his doubt in a grunt.

"Maybe, who knows? But Emily is only charged with the murder of Nadia."

"Be that as it may," said Kate, "we'd like your help. If you could keep the murders and Emily's arrest in the news, it might alert somebody who has some vital information."

"OK."

"Great. It's to your advantage as well, Dale. When we get Emily released you can do a series of articles about it. We'd give you our full co-operation."

"Sounds good. Only thing is, I'll be pretty busy with this profile on Clive Wheatley."

"Clive Wheatley? Who would read that?"

"Everybody's interested in the next bishop of Lovendale."

"What?"

"Have you not heard? It was announced last night."

"Well, I can see what you mean, but the story of the local murders might even run to a book. The fact you had a relationship with one of the victims and were a suspect at one stage would add interest."

"Well, I'd rather not discuss that if you don't mind."

Oh dear, that was a mistake.

"It seems Dawn was having a problem with a guy she'd had a relationship with. Did she tell you about him?"

"No."

"Do you remember her saying anything, anything at all, about anyone she'd been involved with?"

"She never said anything specific, but she kind of joked about other blokes, you know, teasing, like. I remember her saying on one occasion she would be seeing her toy-boy later in the week."

"Any idea who it was?"

He shrugged.

"None of this exactly fit in with her religion, did it?" asked Kate.

"Christianity isn't exactly my specialism but Dawn used to say it was the religion of love. She thought the church was far too hung up on sex."

"Anything else?"

"Look, Kate, I'm willing to help you and Sam, he's my mate, but... you've got to realise I loved Dawn. People talk about the love of my life, and it's become a tabloid cliché, but Dawn really was the love of my life, so it's a bit difficult to talk about other blokes she might have been with."

There was nothing more to be said. As she thanked the *Lovendale Chronicle's* chief reporter, Kate asked herself how long a guy who loved a woman so much could tolerate knowing he was far from the only man in her life.

* * *

Later, Kate opened her door to a youngish woman who looked familiar. She tried and failed to put a name to her.

"Hello."

"Oh, hi. I'm looking for Sam, he's not in and I wondered if he was with you."

"I'm afraid not."

The woman looked Kate up and down before saying more.

"You're Kate, aren't you? I'm Olivia, Nadia's partner."

For a moment Kate was flummoxed then invited her in.

"I'm sorry about Nadia," she said once they'd gone into the living room and sat down. "It must have been a terrible blow."

Olivia nodded in acknowledgement. She was an attractive woman with her expertly styled dark hair and perfect figure.

"How's Sam?" asked Olivia.

"Pretty devastated actually."

"I guess he would be. I couldn't believe it when I heard Emily had been arrested. I've heard you're investigating Nadia's murder. Is that true?"

"Yes. Emily didn't kill her mother."

"I agree. I'd like to help."

"Really?"

Olivia allowed herself the merest of smiles.

"Surprised? Don't be."

"All right, I won't be, but I'm wondering why you want to help."

"Partly for therapy, I suppose, help me get over it. You know, Kate, losing Nadia was bad enough but I learned things about her that just added to the pain. Her drink problem, the affair with that writer, Emily being on the child protection register."

She stopped talking, crossing her legs and linking her hands loosely together, showing perfectly manicured nails.

"I would have said all of that was impossible but, well, it reminded me of the queen in Alice in Wonderland, believing six impossible things before breakfast."

"Literary quotes are the last thing I need, Olivia. It would be useful if I could ask you a few questions."

"OK."

"Right. What did the police ask you?"

"It was a woman who came to see me, I remember. She asked me where I was that afternoon. Of course at that point they knew more than I did. About Keppler and the drinking, you know."

She gasped as if out of breath and wiped tears from her eyes.

"Sorry, I... Anyway, I was walking Horace on the river bank at the relevant time. Lots of people must have seen me."

"Did you know Dawn Fraser or Tiffany Booth?"

"Dawn was a close friend. We taught together for a couple of years. When I first started at Alderton Primary."

"Where were you when Dawn was killed?"

"I was in London with Nadia. I remember hearing about Dawn when we got back."

Olivia seemed to go into a trance for a moment.

"Did you ever have a sexual relationship with Dawn or Tiffany?"

Olivia's mouth dropped open.

"No! Dawn was as straight as they come and I didn't really know Tiffany."

"Anything else you can think of?"

"There was one thing."

"Yes?"

"Well, the morning she read in the *Chronicle* about Tiffany being killed, Nadia told me she'd taken Horace for a walk over towards the cricket pitch the previous night and she'd seen something..."

"Seen something?"

"Yes, I assumed that whatever she'd seen was relevant to the murder."

Kate waited expectantly, looking at Olivia, silently urging her to say more.

"What did she see?"

"She wouldn't say. I think she was scared, to be quite honest. She said, 'There have already been two murders, I don't want to be the next.'"

"Did you tell the police about this?"

She shrugged.

"I did mention it but DC Travis didn't seem interested."

* * *

When Olivia had gone, Kate wondered what or who Nadia had seen. She had gone within yards of the pavilion where Tiffany was found. If she had seen the murderer, that must have been the reason why Nadia herself was killed.

On the other hand, Kate only had Olivia's word for it that Nadia had seen anything. Olivia knew two of the women who had been killed very well, better than most people, but two out of three wasn't enough. The same seemed to apply to all possible suspects. Olivia only had a motive for murdering Nadia. Kate needed to find out who knew all three women, had a motive and was in Alderton at the right time. It was hopeless.

CHAPTER THIRTY-THREE

That night Mark swaggered into the Bricklayers Arms. As he ordered a pint of Carlsberg, he looked over to Brian, glum and overweight on his own at the bar. Propped on a stool, he fed himself from a packet of cheese and onion crisps while nursing a half of bitter. The shopkeeper would always be found in the pub on Wednesday, the night of the weekly darts match. Mark had timed his arrival to ensure he'd have time to talk to Lumley before the players stepped up to the oche.

"Pint, Brian?"

Brian paused from his crisp eating just long enough to answer.

"No thanks. Another bag of cheese and onion wouldn't go amiss."

Mark added the crisps to his order.

"Keeping all right?"

"Not bad."

"Business going OK, is it?"

"Not so's you'd notice."

Brian had always been as cheerful as a wet weekend. Even if he were coining it in, he'd never admit it.

"Gone downhill since I left, has it?" Mark laughed.

Brian frowned at him like a teacher at a wayward pupil. Mark tried to jolly him along, never an easy task.

"Only joking, mate. I always enjoyed working in the shop. I mean, I was only a schoolboy at the time but it stood me in good stead for a career in retail, know what I mean?"

"Hmm."

"You, er, heard about Emily, I suppose."

The pensioner who had replaced Emily behind the bar passed Mark his pint of lager and Brian his crisps.

"Yeah. Bad business."

"Not a happy time in the village, is it? Three murders."

"Best not to think about it."

Mark took a long swallow of his lager.

"How can I not think about it, Brian? My girlfriend's under arrest and I'm drinking in the very pub where she was a barmaid until recently."

"Must be hard for you."

Was Brian getting in touch with his feelings? There was a first time for everything.

"Yeah. You must be upset about poor Tiffany."

Brian tried his best not to react, but his lip curled, Elvis like.

"Not particularly. I mean I'm sorry the girl's dead, must be awful for her mother..."

"Oh, I thought you and Tiff were close."

Brian drank some more and took a crisp out of the bag. He spoke through crunches.

"I wish people would stop saying that."

"Sorry if I upset you, mate," said Mark. "I thought you and Tiff had something going at one time."

Brian replied with well-controlled anger, somehow managing to keep his voice low so that only Mark could hear him.

"There was nothing between Tiffany and me. Nothing whatsoever. OK, we had a fling but that was it. A bit of fun and look what it led to. Police harassing me and all sorts."

Mark drank his lager and worked out his strategy.

"Must have been tough, mate. You need to talk about it, doesn't do to keep things bottled up."

"So they say."

"Did the cops give you a hard time, like?"

Lumley didn't answer straight away, keeping his mouth tight shut and breathing noisily in and out.

"Yeah and all because of that radged prat I was stupid enough to marry."

"How was that, Brian?"

More head shaking followed this question.

"She only announced to everyone in the shop about me and Tiffany, you know..."

"Gerraway."

"So when Tiffany was killed, that Sergeant Penrose was round to see me like a flash."

"Suppose he would be."

"He made some nasty insinuations, I can tell you."

"What sort of insinuations?"

Brian munched his crisps, taking the occasional sip of beer until he was ready to respond.

"He as good as accused me of Tiffany's murder."

"He never did."

"I'm telling you. Said 'Of course if she wanted to end your relationship maybe you attacked her in a fit of jealousy and went too far.' What a load of rubbish. We didn't have a 'relationship', it was just..."

"Casual?"

"That's the word."

"At the same time, Brian, somebody did kill Tiffany."

"Obviously, but it wasn't me. I was in the shop all day when she was killed."

"I know you didn't do it, Brian. Goes without saying. It's just that these three murders are linked, I'm convinced of it. Finding out who killed Tiffany could be the key to getting Emily out of prison."

Brian stuck his hand in the crisp bag only to find it empty. He looked as disappointed as a child deprived of sweets. Mark ordered another packet before having another go at Brian.

"Tiffany must have said something crucial to you. Think about it."

"Something crucial?"

"Yeah, you know, was anybody threatening her..."

"Don't think so..."

Useless pillock.

"One thing that struck me about Tiff was how much money she seemed to have."

"Yeah, somebody was giving her stuff, I do know that."

Mark paid close attention.

"Giving her stuff? How do you mean, like?"

"She was always hinting that she had a regular supply of cash and goodies, that was how she put it."

Now for the million dollar question.

"Who was this sugar daddy?"

"I've no idea."

Great. Thanks for wasting my time, Brian.

CHAPTER THIRTY-FOUR

Yawning and scratching her head, Kate went into the hall, thinking 'Monday morning. Another weekend gone. No real progress'. Picking up the mail, she took it into the living room and flopped on the settee, then flicked her way through half a dozen items, mostly junk mail, bills and charity appeals. The only item that stood out was a postcard of Little Moreton Hall in Cheshire. Addressed to 'Dawn, Deputy Head Teacher' it had been forwarded from the school:

> *Hello Dawn*
>
> *Recognise this place? Happy days, eh? I'll be up in your neck of the woods soon. Why don't we meet up?*

The writer gave a mobile number and signed himself *Jonny* with three kisses. Interesting. Kate looked up to the wall clock, trying to work out New York time.

* * *

"Hi, Kate," said Michelle three hours later, "great to hear from you, but I'm pushed for time. Early meeting."

"That's OK, I wanted to tell you about this strange postcard that's just arrived."

Kate read out Jonny's message.

"Oh, my God. Listen, Kate, could you call him, see when he's in Lovendale? I was planning to come home for a few days soon. If humanly possible I'll make it to coincide with this Jonny's visit."

"Right. Should I tell him what's happened to Dawn?"

"Could you?"

It wasn't something Kate was looking forward to, but she agreed.

* * *

"Why not tell us about you and Dawn?" said Kate a week later, as she sat having lunch at the kitchen table with Michelle and Jonny.

They had learned by then that Jonny was an IT consultant from Nottingham. His work took him round the country.

"We met in the tea room of Little Moreton Hall. It was a Friday in mid-April, just after Easter. The place was busy and we had to share a table for lunch. We got talking."

Jonny was tall, good-looking and had a slight Midlands accent. Nobody ate much of the Marks and Spencer's goodies Michelle had bought.

"I liked her from the first, you know. Fancied her too, I guess."

He stopped talking, a faraway look on his face.

"I was heading back to Nottingham after lunch – I'd finished the job I was doing in Congleton. She came home with me and stayed until Monday."

Was that all they were getting? Not if Kate had anything to do with it.

"So, you spent the weekend together and... what? Did you arrange to meet again?"

He shook his head.

"I'd like to have done, I thought she was lovely. Dawn, though, she made it clear this was just kind of an interlude."

Michelle wiped a tear from her eye.

"I'm sorry, Michelle," said Jonny, "this must be hard for you."

"It's OK. I... I, er, feel as if I'm getting to know my sister at last."

"Given Dawn's attitude, what made you get in touch with her?" asked Kate.

"Well, when she'd left that Monday morning I thought, nice while it lasted, you know. Trouble was, I couldn't stop thinking about her. Since my divorce last year, I'd never met anyone I really liked until Dawn."

"I know what you mean," said Kate.

"It took me ages to work out a way of getting in touch. We're so used to texts, twitter and all that stuff, we forget about the old fashioned way. I thought of the postcard. Sadly, I was too late."

He gazed into the middle distance.

"You must have thought you got to know her quite well," said Kate, "what did you talk about?"

"Lots. Our backgrounds, music, books. We were both great fans of Richard Keppler."

Kate and Michelle spoke together.

"Richard Keppler?"

"Yeah, she said she'd met him at a book signing in Lancashire somewhere."

"When was this?"

"Not sure. Last year some time, I think. She was planning to go to another of his readings at a hotel up here."

"Was Keppler one of her lovers?"

"If he was, she never told me about it."

"What else can you tell us? Was Dawn worried about anything?"

He sat back and screwed his eyes up in concentration.

"There was one guy she seemed a bit unsure of, almost scared."

Kate and Michelle exchanged a glance.

"What did she say about him?" asked Kate.

He shrugged.

"It's hard to remember everything," he said. "They'd had a bit of a fling and she wanted to finish it. He wouldn't take no for an answer."

Jonny thought for a moment, rubbing his chin.

"He kept going round to her house uninvited, calling her mobile. He apparently used a cheap pay-as-you-go phone so his calls to Dawn couldn't be traced to him."

"The police said her phone had gone missing," said Michelle.

"Yes, they did. Just one more thing, Jonny, where was he from, this stalker?"

"I don't know exactly. From round here, I think... yeah, that's right, she said he was an important man in the locality."

Kate was quick with her next question.

"Important?"

"I can't be sure that was the word she used. Something like that anyway: influential, well-known..."

"At the time you were talking to Dawn, was this man still a problem?"

"Oh, yes."

* * *

When Jonny had left, Kate thought about Dawn and all her men. Dale Wilson, for example, was in a similar position to Jonny but at least he got to see his loved one more than once. Why did Dawn do it? Was she looking for new experiences or making up for lost time? Dawn had known or at least met Richard Keppler, who now had a connection to at least two of the three women who had been killed. And she had been given a tantalising glimpse of the so-called stalker. Who was the 'important' man who had been harassing Dawn? Was he her murderer? It could mean a breakthrough or another blind alley.

CHAPTER THIRTY-FIVE

"I'm going to give up writing about crime, Kate, try something lighter," said Richard Keppler.

He was still staying in the holiday apartment where he had found Nadia's body.

"I'm not interested in your literary ambitions," snapped Kate. "This isn't fiction. It's all too real and we're both in the middle of it. I've come round here today to ask for your help."

He nodded. Kate moved on to the point of her visit.

"Emily is innocent. I'm talking to anybody who might have information that helps with Emily's defence. There is evidence that you knew at least two of the women who have been murdered."

Judging by the startled look on Keppler's face, the statement had hit home.

"What are you talking about? Which two women?"

Kate paused, letting him stew.

"Nadia Harding and Dawn Fraser."

"Dawn who?"

Was there a second or two of hesitation there?

"Fraser. She was the first of three women killed in Alderton recently."

"Terrible, but..."

"You were in Lovendale around the time Dawn died."

"Hey, what is this?"

Kate proceeded logically to the next point. In contrast with Keppler she was calm and in control.

"The same applied to Nadia."

He tutted.

"I can hardly deny knowing Nadia but I didn't know Dawn Fraser."

Time for explanation.

"You met Dawn during a book signing last year and again not long before she died. She bought one of your books on both occasions. She was quite a fan apparently."

"I'm glad to hear it, but I'm sorry to say I can't remember Dawn."

"You sure?"

"Positive. I do quite a few signings."

"Let me jog your memory. She was early forties, blonde, rode a motorbike…"

Recognition showed in Keppler's eyes.

"Yes, I do remember her now. She came to the Carpenters Arms event in her leathers. Made quite an entrance. I'd forgotten the name."

"Anything you do remember about her?"

He shrugged.

"Not really... although no, there was something. After I'd signed her book, she went off to get a glass of wine and a guy came up to her."

"A guy?"

"Yeah, he tried to talk to her but she wasn't having any."

This could be promising.

"What exactly happened?"

"She turned away from him, he took hold of her arm, she said something in a kind of stage whisper. Get lost or maybe something stronger. I don't think anyone else noticed, but I'm always on the lookout for promising material."

She nodded.

"What happened next?"

"I was distracted so I couldn't say. When I looked over again to where they'd been arguing, they'd both gone."

"What did the man look like?"

"Difficult to say. There were a few people in my line of vision. I had a clear view of Dawn but not of him."

"God, this is so frustrating. You must have seen something. Colour of hair, clothes?"

He shook his head.

"A dark jacket, I think... nothing really registered."

Despairingly, she thought of all the men in Lovendale who owned a dark jacket.

"Getting back to Dawn herself, you didn't sleep with her?"

He held his head in his hands.

"For God's sake. I would have remembered if I'd... No, I didn't sleep with her. What are you getting at anyway?"

"Well, Dawn had sex with a lot of guys over the past couple of years so it wouldn't be a complete surprise if she came on to her favourite author."

"She didn't."

After another five minutes of questioning, during which Keppler denied all knowledge of Tiffany Booth, Kate left. The more she and Mark found out, the more they needed to know. Had they bitten off more than they could chew? Even if they had, there was no question of giving up. Mark wouldn't allow it for one thing.

* * *

Kate couldn't believe her luck when she bumped into Ed Fraser the next morning. She was just leaving M&S in Loventon.

"Hi, Ed, how nice to see you again," she lied.

"Oh, hello, er..."

"Kate."

He looked even more shabby than the last time she'd seen him. His jeans hadn't been washed for a while and nor, judging by the smell, had his body.

"I was just about to have lunch, care to join me?"

"In here?"

He gestured towards M&S.

"No, I was thinking of the Market Tavern."

The idea of alcohol did the trick.

"All right then."

Five minutes later Ed was guzzling a pint of Guinness.

"Nice pub this," said Kate, looking up from the menu. "I expect you've been here a lot over the years."

He put his glass down, wiping froth from the wispy apology of a beard he'd decided to grow.

"Yeah, I used to come in a fair bit before I was married."

Kate sipped her mineral water.

"I thought you'd been here more recently."

Alarm ran across his face as he picked up his Guinness again.

"No."

Kate let the silence build.

"Well, Ed, I had hoped you'd be a bit more honest and I wouldn't have to do this."

"Do what?"

She sighed, putting more effort into it than strictly necessary.

"Confront you with your lies."

He slammed his glass on the table, splashing some of its contents on the back of his hand.

"Who are you calling a liar?"

"You denied being in Loventon since you left Dawn in the lurch, but one of the staff in this pub recognised you as the drunk who was thrown out of here around the time Dawn died."

Looking shamefaced, he swigged his drink and looked away.

"You may as well admit it, Ed, you must have told the police you were here."

"What makes you think that?"

He was sounding like a guilty teenager now.

"Because I can't see you withstanding even the most gentle of interrogation."

"What's it to you any road?"

"Emily Flint, your friend's daughter, has been arrested for a crime she didn't commit. I'm helping her solicitor gather evidence to prove she didn't do it."

He drained his glass.

"What's that got to do with it?"

"The same person killed Dawn, Tiffany and Nadia. The police agree Emily couldn't have committed all three crimes so I'm investigating each one in turn."

He shrugged.

"So?"

"When you came to Lovendale at the end of May, did you see Dawn, can you tell me anything that might be relevant?"

At this crucial point the waiter, who looked about seventeen, arrived.

"Can you bring my friend another pint, please? I won't be able to stay for lunch, I'm afraid, I've just remembered an appointment."

When the young man had gone Kate repeated the question.

"I'll tell you what happened, right. After getting made redundant, I was in a bad way. It hit me hard, I don't mind telling you."

"Understandable."

"I was depressed, drinking too much, gambling in the hope a big win would solve my money problems."

The waiter brought Ed's second drink, which he seized in both hands and drank from before continuing.

"I thought about all the mistakes I'd made in my life. Maybe I should never have left Dawn. That was when I decided to go and see her, tell her my troubles. She was always good at sorting things out."

"Until somebody killed her."

"Yeah."

"What happened next? After you realised Dawn might help you?"

"I came up here, fixed up to stay with a mate – I'm still lodging with him actually. I was hoping Dawn would agree to put the house up for sale. Split the proceeds, give myself a nice lump sum, help me start again."

"Why should Dawn do that?"

"Why not? Failing that, she might lend me a few quid until I got back on my feet, take me back even."

So, as soon as things went wrong, he thought of Dawn. He really was useless.

"Did you see her?"

He shook his head.

"No. I got here on a Friday night and was gonna go and see her straight away, but I went for a few pints with my mate instead. Well, I got completely bladdered. On the Saturday afternoon I went round to Dawn's house. She wasn't in. One of the neighbours said she was away so I went back to Sheffield."

Kate looked hard at Ed.

"Dawn dying was good for you, wasn't it?"

"Good? Never. I was gutted when I heard what happened."

"You've inherited a house and all Dawn's worldly goods. A good motive for murder, I'd say."

* * *

"We really need to take stock, Mark," said Kate later that day.

"Yeah."

He seemed strangely quiet as they sat in the office of *Lovendale Cottages* with cups of tea. They had brought their notebooks.

"There's just so much information," said Mark, "too much. How are we ever going to make sense of it?"

My God, if Mark was losing hope they were really struggling.

"Stick with it, Mark. We've set ourselves a big task, but we can do it."

She looked at her notebook.

"Amongst all this stuff there's a fact, an inconsistency, a lie that could prove crucial. We have to find it."

"Yeah, but most of this is probably irrelevant. You know, Kate, I have this terrible fear Emily will spend the rest of her life in prison."

"You mustn't think like that."

They discussed what they had discovered, speculated on possible suspects, searched in vain for somebody with a strong motive who was at the scene of all three crimes at the right time. As Mark was thinking about leaving, Kate's phone rang.

"Hello, Dale... yes, tomorrow's fine... really? I'll look forward to it."

When the call was over, Kate explained to Mark.

"That was Dale Wilson, he's got some news."

"What news?"

"He'll tell me tomorrow evening. He wants me to meet him at six o'clock at the Lovendale Chronicle office in Loventon."

"I'll be there."

* * *

Later, Kate sat on the river bank opposite Michelle's house and tried to make sense of everything. She felt so sorry for Emily and Mark, two young people who had got caught up in a murder case. Neither had a mother to talk to. She and Charles could certainly have had a child of

Emily's age had they not put off all thoughts of parenthood until they had built up their careers. Too late now.

Mark's fear about Emily going to prison was quite rational. She was all too aware of the sentencing options if Emily were to be found guilty. A life sentence with a suggested minimum term to be served would follow a murder conviction. If the court decided she was mentally ill – and, given the background, they well might – she would be committed to a secure hospital. It all seemed so cruel and pointless.

CHAPTER THIRTY-SIX

"Come on, Dale, what's this all about, mate?" asked Mark

Now he and Kate were sitting round a desk in the reporter's poky office, Mark could hardly wait for Dale to tell them his news.

"For the past two days, I've been in the village of Winwood, near Leicester researching my profile of Clive Wheatley. Got back last night."

"Yeah?"

"Clive was vicar there before he came back to the North East. I chatted to the locals and got mostly bland platitudes about what a great bloke he was."

He turned over to the next page in his notebook.

"In the local pub at lunchtime yesterday, a young lad in his early twenties sidles up to me all confidential, like. Asks me to call round to his house."

"Make a meal of it, why don't you?"

"Shut up, Mark," said Kate. "What did this man say?"

"Well," said Dale, "after swearing me to secrecy – I'm not allowed to divulge his name to anyone – he told me Clive got his teenage sister pregnant."

Mark reacted straight away.

"Clive? You're joking."

"It's no joke. This girl was going to Clive for Spiritual Renewal sessions..."

Again, Mark couldn't contain himself.

"Spiritual Renewal? That's a new name for it."

"The powers that be in the C of E frown on that sort of thing. Their first instinct was to hush it up of course. The girl was sent to Coventry – literally – to stay with her gran. Clive found there was a vacancy in his home area.'

"Nice and convenient," said Kate, "but what happened to the mother and baby?"

"Ah. Now we come to the interesting bit. Clive and Penny agreed to care for the child as their own. So little Jacob is Clive's biological son."

"Gerraway," said Mark.

"The girl has been depressed ever since, according to her brother. She's even thinking of trying to get the kid back. Jacob has never been officially adopted. Now for the really interesting bit. My informant told me a blonde, northern woman drove into Winwood on her motorbike."

"Dawn?"

"Yes. And he told her all about Clive's love child."

"If this is true," said Kate, "Clive fits the bill as someone with influence in the community who has something to hide."

"And he might have been up to his old tricks round here."

"Agreed, but in a way all this just complicates things further. Clive may be another suspect for the murders but there are plenty of them. And we can't place him at any of the crime scenes."

"Can't we?"

"Take the day Dawn was killed for example. Clive was in the Carpenter Arms in Bentley. Sam saw him there. Paddy McCann was there as well. Clive swung a punch at him."

Mark thought for a moment.

"What time did Sam see Clive?"

Kate pulled out her phone and dialled.

"Hi, Sam, just wanted to check something. You remember when you saw Clive Wheatley try to punch Paddy? Well, can you remember what time it was?... It might be important... about eight o'clock?... they'd just finished a game of golf... right... no, no, it's... I'll explain when I see you... take care... bye."

"If they'd finished a round of golf by eight," said Mark, "they must have started at four o'clock. Dawn was still alive then."

"How do you know how long a golf game lasts," asked Kate, "are you a golfer?"

"No but I once had a game with my gaffer, trying to keep in with him, you know. Talk about boring. The only thing I remember was how long it took."

* * *

The next morning Kate got up early to type up and print what she had found out so far. She was about to read the lengthy document when she stopped. Sitting back in her chair, she looked at the mass of paper on the table and realised she would not have time to read through the facts, ideas and lists before she had to go to work. Nor could she be truly objective. She needed help from somebody who had played no part in the investigation.

Five minutes later, she was ringing Sam's front door bell. She thrust the document into his hands as soon as he answered.

"Sam, can you read this and tell me what you think? It's a summary of the investigation so far."

Sam looked confused.

"Suppose so, but..."

"Sorry, can't stop or I'll be late for work."

CHAPTER THIRTY-SEVEN

I thought coppers were supposed to hate paperwork, I said to myself as Kate dashed off. Scratching my head, I took the report into the shed and sat at my desk. I had to look for an invoice before I started reading. As I rummaged through the top drawer I came across a school photograph from more than thirty years ago. How did that get in there? Though I had better things to do, I couldn't resist having a look at it.

I was at the front, grinning inanely. On either side of me were Dale Wilson and Clive Wheatley, both looking weird with full heads of hair. What had happened to the other thirty odd smiling ten year olds? Quite a few were still in the village. One of the girls in the back row was now the local GP. I scanned the faces again. I don't know what made me look more closely but when I did, I felt a shock of recognition.

Forgetting all about the missing invoice, I got down to reading the report with renewed enthusiasm. Gradually it began to fit together. The longer I read, the sharper my mind became. I was coming fresh to the investigation so could see what Kate had written objectively. I thought about where various people were at the time of the murders.

I began to focus on the day when Tiffany shoved Rebecca in the village shop, knocking Kate against that freezer. There was no doubt where we all were that day. Too bad that wasn't relevant: it was several days after Dawn was killed and weeks before Tiffany's murder.

As I made my way through the pages, I muttered to myself just like my dad when he was watching the news on the telly and swearing at whichever politician had got his goat on any given day.

"That's not right... that doesn't fit... hang on, that doesn't make sense... no, no, that should be nine..."

It took a long time but at last I had made some progress and was ready to do something. I left the shed and walked to the back door. I stopped to send a text:

> *Hi Kate*
>
> *I've found the answer! Off to do something about it. See you later.*
>
> *Love Sam.*

Before making another move, I hesitated. Maybe I should think about it a bit more. I went back in the shed and re-read Kate's report, taking note of the bits I had underlined. When I had finished, I closed my eyes and let the ideas flow through my brain. I took deep breaths in and out as people, events, snatches of conversation came back to me. Almost everyone I knew had played a part in this drama, but which of them were the important ones?

After a while I was satisfied my conclusions were right. Looking at my watch I realised all that had taken an hour. I went out into the lane at the back of the house. I tried to stay calm. It wouldn't take long to get to my destination but what would I find when I got there?

* * *

"What can I do for you, Sam?" said Clive Wheatley moments later.

He had greeted me like a long lost brother and invited me into the vicarage. I sank down in the shabby settee, looking up at Clive in an old rocking chair. I knew what I had to say to him, it was just a case of getting my ideas in order. Well, there was no point beating around the bush. Just go for it.

"You know Kate's been investigating the murders?"

"I had heard something of the sort."

"She's worked out that the same man killed all three women."

"I've heard that theory before."

He nodded, a half smile on his face.

"This man – the murderer – has something to hide; he has a position to uphold; he doesn't want anyone looking too closely into his personal life."

"I'm not sure how I can help..."

"Kate's investigated lots of people, including you."

He chuckled softly.

"She has my sympathy. There's nothing interesting about me."

"I wouldn't say that. You've had a few adventures. What about the affair with a young woman in Leicestershire?"

"Affair? I don't know what you're talking about."

"You must remember her, Clive. She got pregnant."

Anger flared across his face then was gone.

"Who's been telling you this?"

"It doesn't matter who told me. It was hushed up at the time and ever since you have been terrified someone would find out."

"Well, really..."

"Dawn Fraser found out, didn't she?"

Wheatley swallowed hard and ran his tongue along his bottom lip. He said nothing.

"She threatened to spill the beans unless you agreed to leave her alone."

"Leave her alone? What on earth do you mean?"

"If you insist, I'll explain. You'd had a fling with Dawn but she wanted to end it. You wouldn't take no for an answer."

"Sam, you're..."

"You were practically stalking her. She had to be got out of the way."

He held up his hand as if to silence me.

"So I killed her, is that what you're saying? You seem to forget at the time of Dawn's death I was in Bentley, playing golf at the Carpenters Arms. You saw me in the bar afterwards."

"Partially true, Clive. At first I thought that gave you an alibi but that was based on your having played a full round of golf."

"Well…"

"You tried to punch Paddy McCann so I would remember where you were at the time. But after you'd left us, Paddy McCann told me you and he had only played nine holes."

The vicar pursed his lips. He looked as if he were holding his breath.

"So you must have started around six o'clock. You had time to kill Dawn then get to Bentley for your game of golf."

"Preposterous."

"You seemed to think the women of the parish were yours to do as you liked with. Not just Dawn but Tiffany too. They were both invited to spiritual Renewal sessions."

"Spiritual Renewal is..."

"An excuse for you to get your end away. Now having an affair with Dawn, you might have got away with that, but if anybody found out about the pregnant teenager, that would have scuppered your chances of becoming Bishop."

"Listen, Sam…"

214

"Not to mention you being the father of Tiffany's little boy, Harry."

"How can you possibly know that?"

I thought about the school photo I had come across.

"He's the pot model of you when you were a boy. If that's not enough, I'm sure a DNA test would confirm it."

Clive stared past Sam then focused again.

"OK, you're right," he said, "but I didn't kill anyone."

"You killed three women and you were happy to let Emily spend the rest of her life in prison. God, the hypocrisy of it. You dare to lecture other people about their sex lives when you can't keep it in your pants and you're terrified of being found out..."

I heard someone moving behind me. Before I could turn around to see who it was, I felt a kind of cord tightening round my throat. I struggled to grab the cord in a futile attempt to loosen whatever was cutting off my air supply. I felt myself slipping away.

CHAPTER THIRTY-EIGHT

Kate was standing behind the counter in the *Lovendale Cottages* office when her mobile beeped. She couldn't answer straight away because she was handing over some keys to an old couple from Liverpool. As soon as they left, she opened the message. At first, she was baffled. What was Sam on about? He'd *found the answer*. The answer to what? What did *do something about it* mean? She'd be at work for another hour but at least she could speak to him. She dialled Sam's number. It rang for a while before it went to voicemail. She left a message then sent a text.

Once she had finished her shift, Kate hurried out to Sam's house only to get no answer when she rang the bell. Where had he gone to *do something about it* and what was he planning to do? She told herself she was worrying over nothing but wasn't convinced. Something was going to go terribly wrong.

Where could he be? She could hardly explore the whole village bit by bit and hope she'd find him. One of the neighbours might know but most of them would be at work. She couldn't have said how long she stood there before something reminded her of the one person in Loven Terrace who might just be at home during the day.

Having got no answer at the front door of the vicarage, Kate went around the back and found the door open. When she got into the living room, she saw Penny Wheatley leaning over the back of the settee. The man sitting on the settee sounded as if he were gargling. Clive Wheatley was making his ineffectual way towards the gargling man.

"Penny, Penny," he was saying just loud enough to be heard.

Kate went nearer and realised what was going on. Without really knowing she was doing it, she managed to pull Penny away and fling her to the floor.

Sam's eyes flickered. Struggling for breath, he pulled the twine that had become a home-made garrotte from his throat. In the meantime, Penny had got up and moved to the other side of the settee. Sam turned round and gave Kate a half-hearted smile of recognition. Clive sat next to Sam, asking if he was all right but all Sam could do was cough and splutter. Meanwhile there was still Penny to deal with.

Penny stood up straight, squaring her shoulders. She then launched herself on Kate, who tottered but managed to right herself. Now Penny was trying to manoeuvre the position of her hands so she could attempt a bit more strangling.

Kate pulled on the right sleeve of Penny's hoody. Within seconds Penny landed with a thump on the carpet. Sam pulled his phone out of his pocket. He dialled and passed the phone to Kate.

"Can't speak," he wheezed.

Kate asked for the police and explained why she was calling them.

"Yes, attempted murder," she said, "so get here now."

"Would you care to explain?" asked Kate when she finished the call.

Sam began to speak but a fit of coughing silenced him. Kate looked towards Clive but the vicar remained silent.

The figure on the floor began to stir. Penny sat up and looked around.

"I didn't know you did judo, Kate."

"Well you do now. Sergeant Penrose and his team will be here any time now. Can somebody tell me what the hell this is all about?"

Penny looked at Kate and Sam in turn.

"I might as well explain. It'll pass the time until the police arrive."

She had everybody's attention now.

"On the day Dawn died, she had threatened to tell the whole of Lovendale about her dalliance with Clive and about the girl in Winwood who had his baby. Clive came into the garden to tell me about it when I was in the middle of weeding. I told him to put my luggage in my car and strap Jacob in his seat so I could take him to see my parents. I'd try and deal with his problem later. So off he went. The more I thought about it, the angrier I got. Clive was about to be made Bishop of Lovendale and some slapper was out to ruin it. I wasn't having that."

Penny stood up, then sat down on a wooden chair.

"Without even taking off my gardening gloves, I went in search of Dawn. I'd seen her go into Michelle's house so went round to try and reason with her."

"And?"

"She wouldn't listen. I noticed a cheese wire on the table. I didn't really think about it, I just grabbed hold of the handles and strangled Dawn with it."

Poor Dawn, she was only looking forward to an afternoon of passion.

"I took her phone from the table" Penny went on, "dragged the body to the shed, then left for Leicester. I dumped the mobile in a bin at the motorway services."

"And that was it?"

"Yes. I knew Dawn wouldn't be missed for a while because..."

"She was meant to be going away the next day," Sam whispered, "a few days later you phoned me pretending not to know where Dawn was."

He started coughing and spluttering again.

"Well spotted, Sam. Better late than never."

"Did you know you would be the one to discover the body?" asked Kate.

"Not until Michelle texted me about the jumble in the shed."

"What about Tiffany?"

"Well, a few weeks later Clive came to me for help again. Tiffany had started to demand even more money. Greedy bitch. We'd had to set her up in business, then it was a new phone, new TV, new everything."

There was a short silence, broken only by Sam's coughing.

"I went to the pavilion, where she was working and... well, you know the rest."

"And Nadia?" asked Kate.

"That was when it started to go wrong. Nadia was unfortunate..."

"Unfortunate?"

"Yes, wrong place at the wrong time. She saw me leaving the pavilion after I'd dealt with Tiffany. I was in a hurry to get away and hoped she wouldn't realise the significance of what she had seen."

Penny tapped her fingers on her thighs as if beating out a rhythm.

"The next morning, I was walking through the village. There was a bit of a wind so I was wearing my new hoody, I remember. I was wondering what to do about Nadia when I saw this guy coming out of a holiday apartment on the green. Then I noticed Nadia at the door, seeing him off. I went over and knocked at the door. She let me in, even seemed pleased to see me. I went out the back way."

"After you'd killed her?"

Penny nodded.

"I panicked when I heard somebody ringing the front door bell. As I ran off, I realised I'd dropped the murder weapon."

Just at that moment DS Penrose came in.

CHAPTER THIRTY-NINE

"Well, Sam, I think I've solved the mystery of how Emily's fingerprints got on the murder weapon," said Zoe Troble a couple of hours later.

When DS Penrose had finished with me, I managed to phone Zoe without coughing too much. Now we were in my kitchen, eating fish and chips.

"Hardly relevant now, is it?" I said.

She took her notebook from her bag, flicking through the pages and ignoring my question.

"I like to get things right. Now we know Penny Wheatley lost the murder weapon in the garden of the holiday apartment, it's obvious."

"Not to me it isn't," said Kate.

"I got permission to call Emily as soon as I heard from you. I told her what had happened. After a while she remembered that when she went to the holiday apartment, she'd looked through the back window, saw her mother and thought she was drunk. In her hurry to get away she dropped her handbag on a bench on top of a wood and wire contraption."

"Sorry, Zoe. What's this got to do with anything?"

"Pay attention and you might find out. This contraption got entangled with the bag so Emily picked it up by the wooden handles and chucked it on the ground."

"And that's how her fingerprints got on the murder weapon," I said.

It made sense. Not much else did.

"Anyway," said the solicitor, "I'm gonna do my level best to get her home tomorrow."

* * *

"Thanks for coming to my rescue last night," I said to Kate the next morning, as we sipped tea in my double bed.

"You're welcome," Kate said with a smile.

"That judo was impressive."

"Thanks. That throw's called Yoko Otoshi."

"What, John Lennon's girlfriend?"

She nodded.

"That's the one. Not a lot of people know that."

We grinned at one another as my phone rang on the bedside table.

"Hello... speaking... great... yes... yes, I'll get there as soon as I can."

I punched the air as if I'd scored the winning runs in the Ashes.

"It's official. Emily's being released at two o'clock. I'm going to pick her up. Fancy joining me?"

"You try and stop me."

* * *

A week later, Clive came round. We sat facing one another in the living room. It was hard to say who was the more embarrassed. He was the first to speak.

"I've come to say goodbye."

Right, just say it and you can go.

"I'm going back to Leicestershire with Jacob. He'll be living with his birth mother and I'll be seeing him regularly."

Was I supposed to be pleased?

"I've no idea what I'm going to do there," he went on. "They won't be making me a bishop, that's for sure."

"So I heard."

"I just want you to know I had no idea what Penny had done."

"I'll just have to take your word for it, won't I?"

He nodded.

"She's always been ambitious, you know. Always wanting to… achieve something. When she gave up her job, it was me who had to do the achieving."

I wasn't interested. In a million years, I would never understand what Penny had done and if he was expecting me to forgive her, forget it. Emily was home, that was all I was worried about. Clive kept on talking but soon realised I wasn't listening. He got up to leave.

"Emily's recovering well, Clive, thanks for asking," I said.

"Good."

"Just tell me one thing. Why did you take a swing at Paddy?"

He shrugged.

"I was stressed and Paddy McCann is an annoying sod."

* * *

Three months later Kate and I were walking through the Lovendale Hills, admiring the rich autumn colours and talking about Kate's fortieth birthday party in London next week.

"Not only will it be a great do, you'll be able to see Emily," said Kate.

"Yeah. It sounds as if she's having a good time so far."

I thought back to a week ago when I had taken Emily to London to start university. I was afraid she was saying she was happy down there to stop me from worrying, but didn't voice my concerns.

We walked on in silence while I thought about Emily. Would she be permanently damaged by her time in prison? She'd been through enough trauma before being locked up. Kate's voice broke into my thoughts.

"I've got something to tell you."

"Oh?"

"I've now got a full-time job."

I looked anxiously across to her. Was she going back to London? I didn't fancy that.

"The manager of *Lovendale Cottages* is retiring," she explained, "and I'm taking over from her."

"Brilliant."

"There's more."

"More?"

"I'm going to buy Michelle's house."

That sounded like good news.

"Tell me more."

"She hasn't been able to sell it so she's dropped the price and, well, I do want to stay here."

"Who can blame you? It's lovely."

And so are you, I thought. She took my hand.

"Also," said Kate, "there's this bloke I quite like."

If you enjoyed this book, please let others know by leaving a quick review on Amazon. Also, if you spot anything untoward in the paperback, get in touch. We strive for the best quality and appreciate reader feedback.

editor@thebookfolks.com

www.thebookfolks.com

Also by Bud Craig

The PI Gus Keane trilogy, comprising:

Tackling Death
Dead Certainty
Falling foul

(Available in paperback and on Kindle as *Salford Murders.*)

High Profile

Available only on Kindle

Printed in Poland
by Amazon Fulfillment
Poland Sp. z o.o., Wrocław